The Trial
of Judas Wiley

Also available in Large Print
by Lewis B. Patten:

The Cheyenne Pool
Death Rides a Black Horse
The Killings at Coyote Springs
The Law in Cottonwood
Lynching at Broken Butte
Man Outgunned
Red Runs the River
Ride a Tall Horse
Showdown at Mesilla

The Trial
of Judas Wiley

LEWIS B. PATTEN

G.K.HALL &CO.
Boston, Massachusetts
1984

Copyright © 1972 by Lewis B. Patten

All Rights Reserved

All of the characters in this book are fictitious, and
any resemblance to actual persons, living or dead, is
purely coincidental.

Published in Large Print by arrangement with
Doubleday & Company, Inc.

Set in 18 pt English Times.

Library of Congress Cataloging in Publication Data

Patten, Lewis B.
   The trial of Judas Wiley.

   "Published in large print"—
   1. Large type books. I. Title.
[PS3566.A79T72   1984]   813'.54   84-8918
ISBN 0-8161-3624-6   (lg. print)

The Trial
of Judas Wiley

Chapter I

The minute he opened his eyes it returned, that heavy foreboding caused by his knowledge that today the trial began. Sunlight streamed into the east-facing window of his room. Cottonwood leaves, turned gold by early October frosts, rustled just outside in the morning breeze. Judge Jonas Fuller got out of bed, a tall and gangling man, slightly stooped as though from an unconscious effort to adjust to the lesser height of his fellow men. He shuffled to the window and stared down into the sun-drenched street.

He felt it more strongly now, as though the uneasiness of the town were a real and tangible presence in the street. The townspeople were as aware as he that today Jude Wiley went on trial.

Jonas Fuller would preside over Judas Wiley's trial. Frowning, he ran a hand through his shock of graying hair, mussed from the night's uneasy sleep. Downstairs he could hear his daughter in the kitchen, preparing breakfast. He could smell coffee.

He continued to stare thoughtfully along the dusty street. He didn't know what Solomon Wiley was going to do to save his son. So far, Solomon had acted with highly suspicious mildness. Maybe that was the reason for the town's and Jonas Fuller's uneasiness. Mildness was not part of Solomon Wiley's character.

Wiley might intend to wait and see if the jury acquitted his son, Jonas thought, however unlikely that course of action seemed. Maybe he even intended to abide by the jury's verdict, whatever it might be. But Jonas didn't believe that and neither did anybody else. Solomon Wiley wasn't going to let one of his sons be hanged. And so the whole town waited uneasily to see what he would do.

Jonas shaved, using the pitcher of hot water his daughter had left on the floor just outside his door. He dressed with care and afterward descended the stairs heavily, feeling ten years older than his fifty-seven years.

Susan turned her head as he came into the kitchen. He thought her face was pale. He thought he saw fright in her eyes and he thought her smile was forced. She said, "Good morning, Judge."

He grinned at her. She always called him judge and there was usually a light, teasing quality in her tone. Today that quality was gone.

He sipped the coffee she gave him, watching her. Her paleness and her obvious fright puzzled him. He said, "Don't worry about it so much. It's only another trial."

She glanced at him and forced a smile. She was a pretty girl of seventeen. Her mother had been dead now for eleven years.

Many times he had thought he owed it to her to marry again. A girl should have a mother when she was growing up. But he'd never found anyone and now it was too late. Susan was grown. One of these days she'd bring a young man home and tell her father she was going to marry him. He dreaded it but he knew it was inevitable.

With her back to him, she busied herself at the stove. Bacon sizzled and filled the room with its appetizing smell. She got some eggs

3

out of the pantry and carried them to the stove.

A sudden crash made Jonas start. The eggs lay broken on the kitchen floor. Susan was staring down at the mess, face white, lips trembling.

Jonas got quickly to his feet, surprised to see the sudden tears in Susan's eyes. He said, "Now, now, it's only a few eggs. Nothing to cry about."

As though his words had opened a floodgate, her tears came streaming from her eyes. She put her trembling hands over her face and for a moment sobbed helplessly. When she felt his touch, she whirled, ran from the kitchen and up the stairs.

He stared after her confusedly. He hadn't known the prospect of the trial had upset her so or even that it had deeply affected her.

He moved the pan of bacon to the back of the stove. He cleaned up the broken eggs, refilled his coffee cup and sat down patiently to wait. She would be back after she'd had time to compose herself. She would be contrite. But she still would be upset.

Susan returned, pale, her eyes red from weeping. She said almost inaudibly, "I'm sorry," as she got more eggs from the pantry and broke them into the pan.

Jonas didn't reply. He avoided looking at her for fear she might catch him at it and burst into tears again. She brought his breakfast and refilled his coffee cup. She excused herself and disappeared.

Frowning, Jonas ate. Afterward, he lighted a cigar and puffed it thoughtfully. Susan did not reappear.

Finally he got to his feet. He put on his hat and coat and went out the front door, closing it quietly behind him. He was still frowning as he headed along the street toward the courthouse. Susan's behavior still puzzled him. It wasn't like her to get upset over a trial, even a murder trial. It wasn't like her to get this upset over anything.

Maybe it wasn't the trial at all, he thought. Maybe she just felt trapped. Maybe she wanted to get away, to get married, to begin living a life of her own. He hadn't tried to hold her but he might have done so simply by depending on her so much. He'd have to talk to her about that, he thought. He'd talk to her tonight.

He walked briskly, occasionally nodding or speaking to someone he passed on the street. The frown had disappeared from his face but a little core of worry about Susan still remained. Because he wasn't sure he had correctly guessed the reason for her agitation.

The courthouse sat back from the street, surrounded by lawn and trees. The courtrooms were on the second floor, the county offices on the first. The basement was occupied by the sheriff's office and the jail.

Sam McCool, the sheriff, was visible at his desk through the open door. Jonas descended the half-dozen steps and went inside. "Morning, Sam."

"Morning, Jonas."

For a moment Jonas stood there, hesitating. The sheriff asked, "You want to see me about something?"

Sam McCool was a blocky, solid man, his hair turned gray. He wore a sweeping mustache, also gray and stained with tobacco juice. There was a cuspidor beside his desk. McCool had a daughter the same age as Susan and he was also a widower. Jonas had meant to ask him what he thought of Susan's outburst. Hesitating, he shook his head. "I guess not, Sam." Then he grinned. "Do you ever feel as if raising a girl was more of a woman's job than a man's?"

McCool grinned back at him. "Every day. You got some special problem today?"

"She seems awfully pale. She dropped

some eggs and burst into tears. I thought maybe she felt trapped, taking care of an old man when she'd rather be raising a family of her own.''

Sam McCool said, ''Why don't you let her tell you that? She will, you know, if it's true.''

''I haven't tried to hold her, Sam. But maybe just by needing her I've made her feel . . .''

''You're making trouble for yourself. Girls get upset now and then. Women too. They ain't the same as boys.''

Jonas nodded, feeling better for having unburdened himself. He said, ''Court will convene at ten. Have Jude there ten minutes or so before, will you?''

''Sure.''

''I suppose the whole damned Wiley tribe will be on hand.''

McCool nodded. ''You can count on it.''

Jonas went out into the sunlight again. He climbed the courthouse steps slowly and went into the long, tiled hall. He climbed to the second floor and opened the door leading to his chambers, breathing hard.

It still was not yet nine o'clock. He sat down in his swivel chair and put his feet up on the roll-top desk. He couldn't seem to get

7

Susan off his mind and he couldn't stop worrying.

He got up and began pacing nervously back and forth, trying to compose his thoughts. He was still pacing when Jake Tipton, the bailiff, arrived at nine.

Susan Fuller stood at her upstairs back window, looking down into the alley and into the weed-grown vacant lot beyond. The Fuller house sat virtually alone, with vacant lots on both sides and to the rear. The isolation hadn't used to bother her. Now it did. Ever since Andrew Wiley had paid her a visit a week ago today.

He had come riding up the alley, big, bearded, and dirty, smelling of horses and tobacco and whiskey and of man sweat that had permeated his clothes and grown stale. He had towered almost a foot over her as he stood at the back door looking through the screen. In a voice she had tried to make assured she had said, "The judge isn't here. You can find him down at the courthouse this time of day."

"It ain't the judge I came to see."

That left her at a loss for words. It also stirred a growing uneasiness in her. Wiley went on, "My brother's goin' on

8

trial next week.''

"What has that got to do with me?''

"Nothin', maybe. Maybe a lot.''

"What do you mean by that?'' By now she was thoroughly scared. The screen door was hooked but she knew he could yank out the hook with a single jerk on the door.

"I mean we ain't goin' to stand by an' let Jude be hanged. You tell the judge it would be a shame if somethin' was to happen to you. Like maybe the same thing that happened to the gal Jude is supposed to have killed.''

Susan stared at him, finding it difficult to believe she was hearing Andrew Wiley right. She said firmly, "He killed that girl all right. She said so before she died.''

"She lied. But I ain't goin' to argue it with you. Just tell the judge to see that Jude goes free. Otherwise . . .''

"I'll tell him what you said. And he'll have you thrown in jail.''

To her surprise, Andrew didn't seem worried about that. He said, "If I go to jail, there's still Pa and Matt an' Sime an' Luke an' Tom. They ain't made no threats so they won't go to jail. One of 'em will git you, girl. Take my word for it.''

His eyes were as hard as those of a boar.

9

His smell was overpowering. He stared down at her a moment more, eyes narrowed and threatening. He let his gaze stray downward deliberately, looking her over the way he would a scantily dressed girl in a saloon. Her face flamed and she couldn't meet his eyes. He laughed and the laugh made her chest feel empty, made her heart beat fast with fear. He turned and walked away without another word. He mounted his horse, rode down the alley and disappeared.

She slammed and locked the door. She ran through the house to the front door and locked it similarly. She was trembling uncontrollably, more terrified than ever before in her life.

Her father would know how to handle this, she thought. She would tell him the minute he came home.

Frowning, she sat down in a chair, trying desperately to stop her trembling. How would he handle it, she asked herself. Would he have Andrew Wiley thrown in jail?

Of course he would. But what good was it going to do? As Andrew had said, there still was Pa, Sime, Matt, Luke, and Tom. They were as vicious and determined as Andrew was. In fact, Andrew was probably only delivering a message for the family.

She hadn't told her father when he came home. And because she hadn't, her terror grew with every passing day. She locked the doors the minute her father left the house. Sometimes she barricaded herself in her room, even though she knew they'd do nothing to her at least until the trial began.

She wasn't aware of it, but there had been two courses open to Solomon Wiley. He could have broken Jude out of jail, given him money and let him run away. Or he could let him go to trial and through threats and intimidation, see that he was freed.

The second alternative appealed most to old Solomon because he bitterly hated the people in the town of Canyon Creek. He hated them because they had always looked down on him and his family.

His son had killed Ruth McCracken all right. He'd come home with the marks of her fingernails on his face. But Jude hadn't meant to kill the girl. If she hadn't flirted with him and then treated him like dirt when he took her up on it, she still would be alive. Solomon would get Jude off, if he had to threaten the judge and his family, the sheriff and his family, the jurors and witnesses and their families. And he'd make good on his threats if that was what it took.

11

This morning, there was no movement in the alley behind the Fuller house. Or in the vacant lot beyond. The October sun was warm and bright and the cottonwood leaves rustled in the breeze.

A meadowlark trilled and another answered him. Susan wished she didn't feel so cold. She closed the window and swiftly made her bed. She crossed the hall to her father's room and made his too. She carried the washbasin of water in which he had washed and shaved downstairs.

She worked swiftly, as if work could take her mind away from the chilling threat Andrew Wiley had made a week ago. But work didn't help. Her fear remained.

And she found herself wishing, to her own shame, that the jury would find Jude Wiley innocent. Then and only then would the threat against her be withdrawn. Only then could she sleep peacefully again.

Chapter 2

The Wiley family lived in a canyon eleven miles from the town of Canyon Creek. The creek that had given the town its name flowed the length of the Wiley place, coming off the high rims a dozen miles west of ranch headquarters and twisting down through the rim-walled canyon. It irrigated the grass hay the Wileys raised, furnished them water for domestic use, then continued through a narrow, precipitous canyon to the town of Canyon Creek. It spilled into the Blue River below the town.

There were only two ways into the valley where the Wileys lived. One was by the road that followed Canyon Creek. And since the road was guarded on both sides by high, precipitous rock walls, a handful of men could guard it against an invading army if need be.

The other entrance was at the head of Canyon Creek, a narrow trail that followed the beginnings of the creek down through the sandstone rim. This was the route by which the Wileys took their cattle out on the mountaintop for summer graze. It could be guarded easily by a single man.

The net result of the land's topography was that the Wileys lived in an unassailable fortress twenty miles long and nearly a mile wide. It would support them indefinitely and it could be guarded without putting too great a strain on their available manpower.

Solomon Wiley had sired eleven sons. Two had been stillborn and three had died before they reached the age of five. Six remained and Jude, named Judas because he was the eleventh, was the youngest. Like Judas, the other five had been named after the apostles, Simon, Matthew, Luke, Thomas, and Andrew.

Solomon Wiley thought of himself as a deeply religious man. He read the Bible every Sunday morning to his assembled family in a sonorous, deep, and measured voice. He insisted that they sit and listen quietly, even the little ones. After that they could do as they pleased. Work was forbidden on the

Sabbath at the Wiley ranch.

Solomon did not, however, permit religion to spill over into the remaining six days of the week. He gave the Lord his day and that was all he figured the Lord was entitled to.

His herd had been built upon a foundation of cattle stolen from the Mormons over near Salt Lake. Men had occasionally come looking for their stolen cattle in the valley of Canyon Creek. Some had stayed, buried in unmarked graves that had never been found and never would be found. Others had found the trail into the Wiley fortress closed, guarded by one or more of Wiley's hard and competent-looking sons.

Solomon's first wife died the fifth year after he brought her here. No doctor had been called to examine her, and it was doubtful if the presence of a doctor would have changed anything. There was nothing organically wrong with her. She was just worn out, used up by the land, by childbearing, by the heavy work she had to do and by the demands of her rough, direct, and virile husband. Solomon always said that everything within a hundred yards of the house was woman's work. He wasn't joking. He meant it literally.

His second wife was a saloon girl from

Denver, chosen the way a breeder would choose a mare. She was young, big-boned, and strong. She had breasts the size of cantaloupes and she was as lusty as Solomon. Trouble was, she was barren. She could give him no sons and so he got rid of her after the second year. He took her to Salt Lake and left her, giving her fifty dollars which he said was fifty dollars more than she'd had when he married her. He brought another woman back with him, having married her without bothering to divorce his other wife. He hadn't wanted to waste two trips to Salt Lake and so had gotten rid of one wife and obtained another in a single trip.

Andrew jogged up the road in mid-afternoon on the day he had threatened Susan Fuller in the town of Canyon Creek. He rode slouched and comfortable, seeing nothing ugly in the collection of haphazard buildings that had grown and spread from the single-room log cabin that had been Solomon's first dwelling here.

There were five houses in all, one each for the families of Andrew, Luke, Thomas, Simon, and Solomon. Jude and Matthew lived with their father and his fourth wife, who was Jude's mother. Jude was her only

16

son. Matthew was the fruit of Solomon's union with his third wife. She had died of pneumonia when Matt was two.

The forge was smoking and Andrew knew Solomon was using it. He rode to the blacksmith shop, which adjoined the barn. A horse stood tied there, waiting to be shod. Solomon was working on another one. He had the horse's right front hoof between his leather-clad knees and was nailing on a shoe.

He glanced up. He was a monstrous man, six feet three inches tall. His shoulders were broad and thick, his chest almost unbelievably deep. He always reminded Andrew of a bull. Now, in his late fifties, he had gone to paunch but his paunch detracted in no way from the impression of raw power that he gave.

His neck was thick and short. His beard was red and so was his hair, which grew long and curly over his neck and ears, matching the mat of curly red hair on his massive chest.

In contrast with the rest of him, his legs seemed short. They were bowed from a lifetime of straddling a horse but they were strong enough. His voice was rasping and harsh. "Well?"

"I saw her, Pa. I told her she'd better talk

to the judge an' tell him to see that Jude went free."

"She'll do it?"

Andrew grinned. "She'll do it all right. I never seen a girl so scared."

Solomon nodded again. He said shortly, "Get on up the creek an' help your brothers finish putting up that hay. Next week we'll all have to be in town."

Andrew didn't comment. He turned his horse and rode up the creek toward the stack rising half a mile away.

Solomon finished shoeing the horse. Sweating heavily he began on the second one. He trimmed and filed the horse's hoofs, digging packed manure and mud from around each frog, then carefully trimming it. When he was satisfied, he put a shoe into the forge to heat.

He worked swiftly and competently, shaping the shoes on the anvil, heating them, cooling them, until they fit the horse perfectly. Only when they did, did he nail them on.

Finished, he let the fire die and put the two horses into the corral. He stood, then, looking north toward the towering rims a dozen miles away. He could see the stacker, a Mormon derrick, dumping hay onto the top of the stack. He could see Simon up there spreading hay, tramping it down.

None of Solomon's family had ever been in trouble with the law before but it wasn't because they hadn't broken any laws. They had stolen, and had sometimes killed. Solomon was guilty of bigamy. He knew his sons were guilty of raping Ute Indian women occasionally when their wanderings took them near the reservation a hundred miles south of here.

But he had always cautioned them to watch their step in town. He didn't want a confrontation with the people there because he needed them. He drove his cattle to the railroad in Canyon Creek. He bought his supplies in town.

In fairness to Jude, he had to admit that Jude hadn't meant to kill the McCracken girl. The little bitch had teased him, flirted with him, and tormented him. And when Jude took her up on it after the dance, she had heaped scorn on him. She had called him a smelly, filthy pig. When Jude put his arms around her she had clawed his face.

Jude was big and he was strong. He'd lost his temper, that was all. And when it was over the girl had lain battered and broken on the ground, dying but not yet dead.

If Jude had had any sense he'd have killed her outright, then and there, Solomon thought sourly. Then she couldn't have told the sheriff who it was that had beaten her. But Jude was stupid and he had been scared. He'd left her and come running home.

Solomon turned his glance to the buildings sprawled here in this valley of Canyon Creek. It never occurred to him to see them for what they were, an ugly collection of unplanned shacks.

They were too familiar to seem ugly in his eyes. He had built a good many of them with his own two hands.

Nothing grew in the area surrounding the buildings. No blade of grass, no bush, no tree. Children played in the dust, the games that children play everywhere. They were as dirty and unkempt as their elders and they stared solemnly at Wiley with unblinking eyes.

A herd of shoats rooted in the dirt outside Solomon's kitchen door. He scattered them with a few well-placed kicks. Squealing, they trotted across the yard.

He went inside. Normally he took things imperturbably, pretty much the way they came. But Jude's arrest had worried him because he sensed that if Jude was convicted and executed it would signal more moves by the townspeople and the law against the Wiley family.

Solomon knew how much he and his family were hated, how much they were feared in town. Because they were, he meant to see that Jude went free, no matter what it took. He would intimidate the judge, the sheriff, the jurors, and would make good on his threats if he must.

Having done so, he'd make sure that nothing like this ever happened in town again. He'd see to it that his sons behaved, at least in Canyon Creek. He didn't want to have to tangle with the town a second time.

He opened the door and went into the kitchen. His wife turned her head and looked at him impassively. He said, "Andrew talked to the judge's girl."

"What if her father doesn't scare?" She was a strong-bodied woman with no gray in her coarse black hair. Her face was expressionless but there was something in her eyes that instantly hid itself when he met her glance.

Solomon said, "He'll scare. He knows what happened to that other girl."

"I want to see my son."

"You can see him next week when the trial begins."

She didn't reply to that. He crossed the room and got a bottle of whiskey out of a cupboard. He sat down at the table and pulled the cork with his teeth. He put the bottle to his mouth and drank. After a moment he said, "We're all going in to town when the trial begins."

"Even the kids?"

"Even the kids. We'll leave Matt to guard the trail. We'll leave Luke and his boy to guard the road. The rest of us will go to town."

"Will there be room in the courtroom for all of us?"

He chuckled humorlessly. "We'll make room even if we have to crowd some of them others out." Solomon knew how a court-room packed with members of the Wiley tribe would affect the jurors.

He lifted the bottle a second time. His eyes met those of his wife unexpectedly and this time there was no opportunity for her to hide the hatred in them. Her hatred didn't surprise him. He simply didn't care. As long as she did her work and kept her mouth shut, he didn't give a hoot what went on inside her head.

Solomon Wiley claimed to set a lot of store by his family, but there was no real sentiment in the man. He knew he needed his sons and he knew that he needed their wives and would eventually need their children too. He had no intention of being forced into hiring the help necessary to run this monstrous ranch.

He claimed to be sentimental about his family, but his only sentiment was greed. Greed was behind his determination to get Jude off. He'd preached family solidarity to his sons and their families for years. If he let Jude be hanged, they'd never believe in him again. One by one they'd leave, taking their families. He'd be powerless to prevent the exodus. And in the end he'd be left alone, with this big ranch to run and nobody to help him do the work.

He thought bleakly to himself that Jude wasn't worth saving because he'd probably do the same damn thing again. What Jude was going to have to have when this was over was a wife. So he'd keep his hands off the girls in town.

Chapter 3

At ten o'clock, Judge Jonas Fuller opened the door that led from his chambers to the courtroom. He heard the bailiff say sharply, "All rise," and heard the stir as the occupants of the courtroom got to their feet. He sat down behind the bench and the bailiff said, "Court is now in session. Judge Jonas Fuller presiding. Be seated." There was another stir as everyone sat down.

Jonas stared at the spectactors. The entire Wiley family seemed to be present, from Solomon, the family patriarch, to the youngest babe in arms. Without making an exact count, Jonas guessed there must be forty of them at least. That left precious little room for other spectators, most of whom were standing packed at the courtroom's rear.

Jonas looked at John Gebhardt, the county attorney, and at Norman Kissick, attorney for the defense. "Proceed, gentlemen, with the selection of the jury."

He sat back in his swivel chair, then, listening as the jurors were called, one by one, and briefly questioned by the prosecutor and by the counsel for the defense. His mind followed the questions and the prospective jurors' answers. His eyes studied Solomon Wiley covertly.

Wiley seemed serenely confident. There was no visible worry in the man. His attitude exuded arrogance rather than concern. And that was puzzling. Jude Wiley faced a charge of murder. The deathbed testimony of the victim named him as the guilty man.

The morning dragged on. At noon, twelve jurors had been selected and Jonas recessed the court until two o'clock.

He got up and left the courtroom but not before he had observed the looks that passed between Jude Wiley and his father and brothers as he was led away by Sam McCool.

He walked slowly home for dinner in midday. The sun was hot despite the fact that it was past the middle of October. He realized he was frowning and he admitted that he was worried. He didn't like the Wiley family's confidence. It was as if they knew something he did not.

It was obvious to him the minute he saw her that Susan had been crying again. Her eyes were red and there was a telltale puffiness around them. She was pale and her hands, as she set the table for dinner, were trembling.

He didn't like bringing it up now but he knew he must. He said, "Susan, something's the matter with you. I want you to tell me what it is."

She looked at him with brimming eyes. He got up and held out his arms and she came running into them, weeping uncontrollably. He waited a few moments until the outburst had subsided before he said, "You can tell me, no matter what it is."

Sobbing, she burst out, "It's Andrew Wiley, Pa. He threatened me."

Sudden fury coursed through Jonas Fuller's mind. "Threatened you?" Never in all his years on the bench had anyone been intimidated as a result of a trial being held in his court. That it should be his own daughter . . . that the one threatening her should be a hulking, dirty animal like Andrew Wiley was unthinkable. He tried to make his voice

26

sound calm even though inside he was seething with rage. "Why did he threaten you? What did he want?"

"He wants his brother Jude set free."

For an instant Jonas was too shocked to speak. When he could, he said, "I'll have Sam arrest him this afternoon."

Susan's words came out between sobs, the way they sometimes had when she was a little girl. "He . . . said . . . that wouldn't . . . do any . . . good. He said . . . even if you . . . threw him in . . . jail, his . . . brothers or . . . his father would see that . . ."

"Would see that what?"

"That . . . the . . . same thing . . . happened to me that . . . happened to Ruth McCracken."

Jonas patted her back comfortingly until her sobs quieted. In a voice he tried to make reassuring, he said, "Nobody's going to do anything to you. They're just trying to throw a scare into us. Now put dinner on. And don't worry any more. I'll take care of it."

"You're not going to let him go?"

"What kind of talk is that? Don't you know your father any better than that?"

She smiled wanly. "I'm sorry. I'll get dinner on." She busied herself at the stove.

Jonas made a special effort to see that his

expression remained serene and unworried. But inside he was as agitated as Susan was. The threat was unthinkable but it had been made. Furthermore, he knew the Wiley family meant just what they said. They were capable of carrying out their threat. If Jude Wiley was convicted and sentenced to be hanged, as he surely would be, then Susan would be in mortal danger from the Wiley family.

He could issue a warrant for Andrew Wiley's arrest, of course, and he could have Wiley sent to prison for the threat. But that wouldn't protect Susan from the other members of the family. In fact, if Andrew was sent to prison for the threat, it would increase Susan's jeopardy instead of decreasing it.

There were only two courses open to him, he realized. He could wait until the testimony was all in and then, no matter how damning it had been, could direct the jury to return a verdict of not guilty and set Judas Wiley free. Or he could send Susan east. He could send her so far away that the Wiley family couldn't find her no matter how they tried.

He ate the dinner Susan put in front of him without tasting it or realizing what it was. As he ate, he tried to keep a normal conversation going with her. He knew he failed dismally. He was afraid, and Susan was afraid, and each knew the other was afraid. But even if she knew what was going on inside his mind, he didn't dare admit it to her. He had to pretend to be unworried or she'd break down again.

He always took a nap after lunch and today he didn't outwardly vary that routine. He went upstairs to his room and laid down on the bed. Sleep was, of course, impossible. He stared at the ceiling, anger smoldering in his mind. But his mind was like an animal in a cage, racing back and forth, seeking an exit, a way out of the dilemma facing him.

He supposed he could issue warrants for the entire Wiley family. For the adult males at least. He could have all of them thrown in jail. He could have them all brought to trial.

Except that doing so would be futile. No jury would convict all of them for a threat that Andrew alone had made. They'd be released and then Susan would be in mortal danger once again.

He heard the clock downstairs chime once and knew it was half-past one. He got up, ran his fingers through his graying hair, straightened his tie, put on his coat, and went downstairs.

He smiled at Susan, kissed her on the cheek and went out the front door. From the gate he called back, "No worrying. You hear?"

She nodded, smiling. She would worry, but it wouldn't be as hard for her now as it had been when she was carrying the burden of fear and worry all alone.

He walked slowly toward the courthouse, when possible staying in the shade. No longer did he feel tired. Anger had put enough adrenalin into his veins to make him feel young again. Damn them! Damn their monumental arrogance! Jude Wiley wasn't going free!

Then he thought of Susan and of Andrew Wiley's threat. And he knew that to promise himself Jude Wiley wasn't going free was too pat. It wasn't going to be as simple as that. The danger to Susan was much too real.

At least, he consoled himself, he didn't have to make a decision immediately. Nothing would be done by the Wiley family until the end of the trial and that might be a week away.

Or it might be only a couple of days, he thought. He suddenly felt cold. And he suddenly was more afraid than he had ever been before.

In Canyon Creek, a jury had never been locked up during the course of a trial. They were dismissed at noon and went home for dinner. They were dismissed again when court adjourned for the day and they went home for supper. They reported for duty each morning at a quarter of ten. They were instructed once not to discuss the case with their families or friends. Beyond that no precautions were taken to keep them isolated.

The murder trial of Judas Wiley was no exception to the rule. But had Jonas Fuller known of the threat Andrew Wiley had made against his daughter before adjourning court for dinner that first day, he might have kept the jury together in the jury room.

As it was, the jury dispersed when court adjourned, making their separate ways homeward where dinner awaited them.

William Clay was twenty-six. His wife, Josie, was the same age and they had two children, five and three. The five-year-old was a boy, the three-year-old a girl. Both children were playing in the back yard when Clay reached home.

Like everyone else in Canyon Creek, Clay knew that Ruth McCracken had accused

Jude Wiley of beating her before she died. He knew about the scratches that had been on Jude's face when the sheriff arrested him. It was damning evidence as far as Clay was concerned. He didn't know what Jude's lawyer could say in his defense. Yet he was trying to keep an open mind because that was what Judge Fuller had told the jury it must do.

He stepped into the kitchen, assailed immediately by the sour smell of sweat, stale tobacco, and whiskey breath. He was startled to see that besides his wife, three men were in the room, all members of the Wiley family. Andrew, Simon, and Thomas were sitting at the table eating what was to have been Clay's dinner. His wife was standing by the stove, white-faced and scared.

Clay felt an instant surge of anger. "What are you doing here?"

"We came to see you, Clay."

"What about?" Clay worked as bookkeeper for Gunther Levy, a cattle buyer. Levy had never bought cattle from the Wiley family and it was doubtful if he ever would.

"About the trial. We came to tell you Jude ain't guilty of killing that girl. Oh, they had a fuss all right an' she clawed his face, but she was fine when he left her to come home."

Clay said, "If he's innocent, he'll be able to prove it in court."

Simon Wiley said, "Nice family you got, Clay. Pretty wife, healthy kids."

Clay understood immediately what they were getting at. He opened the pantry door and reached through. When he turned, he had a double-barreled shotgun in his hands, a gun he used for hunting in the fall. The gun wasn't loaded, but the Wileys had no way of knowing that. He thumbed the hammers back with a double click. "Get out of here. Get out and don't come back. Sam McCool is going to know about your threats."

"What threats? We ain't made no threats. All we did was accept your wife's invitation to dinner an' tell you what a nice family we thought you had."

Clay's knees suddenly began trembling. He shrilled, "Get out! Before I shoot!"

The three big men got up from the table and shuffled to the door. They went out, each looking back as he did, grinning. Clay knew they had seen his shaking knees and the knowledge made him furious.

He put the shotgun down. He went to the door and looked out. The Wileys were talking to the kids, who stood, wide-eyed and scared, like rabbits poised to run. Clay opened his mouth to call the Wileys back, then closed it without doing so.

His wife ran sobbing into his arms. She cried, "Oh, Will, I was so scared. They just came to the door and pushed in and made themselves at home. I didn't know what to do!"

"You did all right." He tried to sound unconcerned. "Is there anything left to eat?"

"I think so. I can fix the children something after you've gone back to court."

William Clay had never had a physical encounter with anyone in his life. His was a life of books and figures. He said unbelievingly, "They were threatening me!"

"They want you to say that Jude Wiley isn't guilty of killing Ruth McCracken, don't they?"

"That's what they want."

"Are you going to do it?"

"No I'm not! I'm going to listen to the evidence and then I'm going to do what I think is right."

"Will they . . . ?" She stopped, her chin quivering.

"Will they what?" But he knew what she meant. He knew she wanted to know if the Wileys would hurt either her or the kids.

She finished, "Will they hurt the kids?"

He shook his head, even though he wasn't sure. "It's just a bluff. They wouldn't dare do anything."

His wife seemed relieved. He sat down at the table and pushed aside the dishes the Wileys had been using. She gathered them up and carried them away. She wiped the table and set it again for him. There was some beef stew left, and fresh bread that she had baked yesterday. He wasn't hungry but he forced himself to eat.

Clay had never thought much about courage, one way or another. It had never been demanded of him before. Nor did he think about it now. What he thought about was justice and the law. And how the system would become a mockery if the jurors allowed themselves to be intimidated by the families of the accused.

He finished eating and went out into the yard. The children came running to his arms, still scared, he knew, by the visit of the three big, bearded, dirty men.

He hugged them to him, wavering. How could he risk the safety of these helpless children?

He'd talk to Sam McCool. He'd ask the sheriff what he ought to do. Yet even as he thought it, he knew it wouldn't do. McCool would tell him the Wileys were bluffing. He might even insist that Clay sign a complaint.

But were they bluffing? As he straightened, he knew that was a chance he could not afford to take.

Chapter 4

The trial convened again at two. The opening statements were brief. John Gebhardt said the state would prove that Judas Wiley murdered Ruth McCracken because she resisted him. He called it murder in the first degree, and asked for the death penalty—by hanging at the state penitentiary at Cañon City. Jude Wiley, listening, turned a little pale when he mentioned hanging. He glanced at his father. Solomon Wiley nodded at him as though to say, "It's all taken care of, Jude."

The defense attorney, Norman Kissick, got up next. He was a young man, only a year out of law school, and this was his first court case. He was plainly scared. He said his client, Jude Wiley, was innocent. He admitted that Jude had quarreled with the dead girl, but said the girl had been alive when Jude went home. He didn't mention what evidence, if any, he would present to support Jude's claim.

Both opening statements consumed less than half an hour. Kissick was just sitting down when Jonas Fuller heard the fire bell.

He wanted to get up and hurry to the window. Instead, he looked at the bailiff, Jake Tipton, who immediately got up and went instead. Tipton turned, his glance finding William Clay. "Looks like it might be your house, Bill."

Before Clay could rise, Jonas Fuller said, "Court will recess until ten o'clock tomorrow."

The words were hardly out of his mouth before Bill Clay was up, crowding out of the courtroom at a run. Jonas looked at Solomon Wiley. There was no giveaway smile on Wiley's face, but his glance met that of Jonas challengingly.

Jonas knew Solomon Wiley was responsible for the fire at Bill Clay's house. In his mind, he checked off Solomon's sons. Three had been with Solomon during the morning session. Only two were with him now, Andrew and Thomas. Simon was missing.

Sam McCool was trying to get out of the

courtroom, battling the crowd that had jammed the doors. Jonas shouted, "Sam!"

McCool turned his head. Jonas beckoned to him. McCool hesitated, plainly wanting to get away, to get to the fire as quickly as he could. Jonas beckoned again, more urgently.

With a resigned shrug, Sam McCool turned and pushed through the group separating him from the judge. He stood below the bench, looking up impatiently. "I ought to be at that fire, Jonas."

"You can go out through my chambers. I suspect that fire was set. Furthermore, I believe that Simon Wiley is the one responsible."

"Are you serious?"

Jonas nodded grimly. "Find out where Simon was this afternoon."

"Why would . . ." McCool stopped, shock apparent in his face. He breathed, "Bill Clay is on the jury. Is that what you're getting at?"

Jonas nodded. He opened his mouth to tell McCool that Andrew Wiley had threatened Susan, then closed it abruptly without saying anything. McCool stared at his face a moment, waiting, knowing the judge had intended to say something else. When nothing was forthcoming, he asked hurriedly, "Is that all, Jonas?"

Jonas Fuller nodded. Sam McCool flung open the door to the judge's chambers and hurried through.

The courtroom was empty now. The fire bell clanged continuously, its sound diminishing as it got farther away from the firehouse. There was a loud murmur outside in the hall, that of many voices. Jonas thought it was notable that the Wiley family had waited and left the courtroom last.

Jake Tipton was waiting, looking at the judge. Jonas said, "Let's go, Jake. Let's see how bad it is. I hope to God that Josie and the kids got out before it was too late."

He went through his chambers, leaving his robe there and picking up his coat. With Jake beside him, he hurried along the street in the direction of the boiling pillar of smoke.

Jonas felt short of breath before he had gone a block. He said, "Slow down, Jake. I'm not as young as I used to be."

"Sure, Judge. Sure." Jake slowed. He studied Jonas's face a moment and then he asked, "You all right, Judge? You feel all right?"

Jonas nodded. There was nothing wrong with him. He felt lightheaded. He was out of breath. His heart was pounding inside his chest, but that was from hurrying. He said, "I'm all right, Jake. We were just walking a little too fast is all."

They turned the corner. Ahead, Jonas could now see the blazing house. The fire was worst at the rear, but it was spreading rapidly to the front. It looked like half the town was gathered in the street out front. The fire engine, to which were harnessed two teams of dappled grays, was pumping water through a hose onto the roof and into the windows, which had been smashed. Smoke came from its boiler stack.

Jonas looked for William Clay, for his wife Josie and for the two little kids. He breathed a sigh of relief when he saw Bill with the children in his arms, with his wife Josie beside him on the front lawn of the house. At least no one had been hurt.

He glanced back in the direction from which he just had come. The Wiley family made a crowd all by themselves, the children leading excitedly, wanting to get to the fire before the excitement of it died. Jonas looked for Simon and saw him, a step behind Solomon.

Sam McCool apparently saw Simon too. He walked to meet the Wiley family and talked briefly with Solomon and then with Sime. Jonas could guess what Solomon's story was. Simon had gone to the outhouse. He'd been waiting out in the hall to come in again as soon as there was an opportunity to do so without interrupting anything. It was a story the Wileys couldn't prove. Neither could it be disproved. Unless someone had seen Simon near the Clay house. And that didn't seem very likely since everyone who wasn't busy elsewhere had been at the trial.

Jonas moved a little closer to William Clay. He suspected that Clay had been threatened just as Susan had. Clay had probably told them to go to hell and this was their way of proving to him how deadly serious they were. He watched Clay as the man turned and saw the Wileys approaching him.

Clay's face turned white. His lips compressed and his jaws clenched hard. He started to put the children down, raw fury in his eyes. And then, as suddenly as it had appeared, his fury disappeared. He lowered his glance from the Wiley family. Flushing, he turned away.

There had never been much doubt in Jonas's mind that the Wileys had set fire to Bill Clay's house. He believed, furthermore, that the Wileys had threatened Bill. Now he was sure of it. Clay was obviously afraid and the Wileys had made their point. Clay would hold out for acquittal and Judas Wiley would go free. Jonas was ashamed of the sudden relief he felt because decision had been taken out of his hands.

In spite of the efforts of the hard-working volunteer firemen, the fire continued to spread into the front part of the house. The pumper ran out of water and clanged away to get some more. But Jonas could see it was no use. The Clay house could not be saved. The fire had too good a start.

The engine was gone for more than fifteen minutes. When it returned, the whole house was ablaze. The firemen were forced to content themselves with wetting down the adjoining houses to keep them from catching fire from the heat.

Jonas could hear Josie Clay weeping. The children were crying too. Clay was trying to comfort them. Jonas crossed the lawn to him. "I'm sorry, Bill."

Clay looked up. There was an awful bitterness in his eyes as he said, "This fire was set, Judge."

"How do you know? Did Josie see anyone?"

Clay shook his head. He started to say something, then glanced at the Wileys and changed his mind. Jonas said impulsively, "I'll get an alternate to take your place on the jury, Bill." He was sorry the minute the words were out.

For a moment he thought Clay was going to be hysterical. The man started to laugh, then doubled and began to sob. He controlled himself with an effort. He looked at the judge and said, "Then it was all for nothing. It cost me my house and now I'm not even on the jury any more."

Jonas couldn't ignore the implication. He said, "Are you telling me that the Wileys threatened you?"

For a moment, he thought Clay would come right out and accuse the Wileys. He glared in their direction.

Then he looked at his house, virtually destroyed. He looked down at his wife and at the tear-streaked faces of his two children. He glanced back up at the judge and shook his head. "Oh no you don't. You don't get me into this any deeper than I already am. I'm off the jury. That's fine. Now all I've got to do is rebuild what I've lost. If I'm lucky, I can do it in another six or seven years. At least my wife's all right and so are my kids."

Jonas discovered that he couldn't meet Bill Clay's glance. He turned and walked away.

The Wileys were clustered on the walk across the street from the burning house. The older members of the family watched impassively as the remainder of the house went up in smoke. The children played in the dust of the street, having already lost interest in the fire which had diminished to little more than a pile of charred and smoldering embers.

Jonas Fuller discovered he could not look squarely at Solomon Wiley either. He hurried up the street toward the courthouse.

He ought to do something. He *had* to do something. But what was he going to do? He didn't dare defy the Wileys because doing so would put Susan in jeopardy. He didn't dare stop the trial, or declare it a mistrial for the same reason.

He wondered how many of the other jurors had been threatened, how many would be threatened before this was over with.

He went to the courthouse but he did not go upstairs where his chambers were. Instead he went into the sheriff's office in the basement and sat down to wait. He took a cigar out of the pocket of his coat, bit off the end and lighted it.

Sam McCool came in around four o'clock. There was a smudge on his forehead and his hands were black. He went to the washstand and began washing them, giving Jonas a nod and a short, "Howdy, Jonas."

Turning, wiping his hands with a towel, he said, "That fire was set, all right. Clay's wife and kids weren't even home at the time and Josie swears the stove was almost cold."

Jonas nodded. "Find anything that would prove us right?"

"Not a damned thing!" McCool said disgustedly. "That's how I got so dirty, looking around for a coal oil can."

"What did Solomon say when you asked him where Simon was?"

"Said he went to the outhouse and was waiting in the hall until he could come back in without interrupting anything." He stared at Jonas, frowning now. "What are you grinning at?"

"I told myself that would be the story they told. When I saw you talking to Solomon."

McCool said, "The hell of it is, I can't prove that Simon wasn't where his old man says he was. Nobody saw him in the hall. Nobody saw him at Clay's house or anywhere."

Jonas said, "The Wileys threatened Clay. He denied it, but I know they did. I excused him from the jury."

"Want me to arrest 'em?"

Jonas shook his head. "Wouldn't do any good. They'd deny it and Clay would refuse to testify."

"What about the other jurymen? If Clay's off the jury, Solomon will go after the others."

Jonas said, "That's why I'm here. I want you to watch Solomon and his sons."

"I haven't got enough men for that."

"Deputize some. Just for tonight. Tomorrow night I'll put the jurymen up at the hotel. I'll keep them isolated so the Wileys can't get to them."

Both precautions were useless, Jonas knew. Even if he kept the Wileys away from the jurymen, the damage was already done. He himself had been threatened, through Susan. He couldn't let Jude Wiley hang. As long as Jude's father and brothers were free, he didn't dare let Jude Wiley hang.

Chapter 5

Sam McCool watched Jonas Fuller climb the steps. He went to the window and watched as the judge crossed the lawn in the direction of his home. The judge walked heavily, his eyes fixed on the ground in front of him.

McCool had been friends with Jonas Fuller for a long, long time. He knew Jonas was troubled. He frowned faintly, raising a hand to tug at the right side of his mustache, which drooped more than did the other side.

Like Jonas, he was sure Bill Clay's house had been set on fire deliberately. But unless he found someone who had seen Simon Wiley in the vicinity, he'd play hell proving it.

Something hanging in the back of his mind kept nagging him, kept the frown upon his face. Jonas was acting strangely. That was what bothered him. And Jonas was apparently having some kind of trouble with his daughter too.

The thought hit him suddenly, like a blow. If the Wileys had threatened Clay—if they had gone so far as to burn down his house to show him how serious they were, wasn't it possible they had also threatened the judge? Or, more likely, that they had threatened Susan as a way of getting the judge to do what they wanted him to do?

He began to pace nervously back and forth. A threat against Susan would explain her agitation yesterday. If the judge knew about it, it would explain his certainty that the fire at Clay's house had been set. Unless Jonas had possessed some knowledge McCool didn't, he wouldn't have been so sure.

He found a cigar, bit off the end and lighted it. He puffed furiously until the office was blue with smoke. If jurors and judge had been threatened, the trial of Jude Wiley would be a travesty, a farce. There was no use going on with it.

But if Jonas did go on with it and if Jude was found innocent, he could never be tried on the same charge again. It was called double jeopardy.

He opened the door that led to the cells. Jude Wiley was the only one in jail. McCool called, "You want anything special for supper?"

Jude didn't answer him. McCool closed the door again. Jonas had told him to round up some deputies and watch the Wileys so that they couldn't threaten any more of the jurors tonight. He supposed he'd better get busy doing it.

He locked the office door and walked across the courthouse lawn. He always kept a horse standing tied to the hitching post in front of the courthouse. He seldom needed the animal but he knew if he ever did need him, he'd need him bad. He untied the reins and mounted, turning the horse toward the north part of town.

Suddenly and unexpectedly, he dug his heels into the startled horse's sides. He lashed the horse's rump with the reins. The animal broke into a lope and McCool guided him toward home. The sudden thought had struck him that if the Wileys could threaten Judge Fuller through his daughter, then he, as sheriff, was also vulnerable.

He slid from the horse before the animal came to a complete stop and ran up the walk to the door. He burst inside, yelling, "Mary!

Mary, where are you?"

She appeared in the kitchen door, startled and, he thought, a little bit frightened too. "I'm here, Pa. What is it? What's the matter?"

He skidded to a halt. He asked, "You seen any of the Wiley bunch?"

"The Wiley bunch? Why in the world would I see any of them? I haven't been downtown since the trial began."

"Don't you go down there, either. Don't you go down there."

"Pa, what in the world are you talking about? What's the matter with you?"

He studied her face for a long, long time, seeing only puzzlement and confusion there. He felt himself relax. He grinned at her. "Nothing. Nothing's the matter with me."

Mary put her hands on her hips and stared at him exasperatedly. "You do beat all. You come storming in here yelling at me and then all of a sudden you calm down and say nothing's the matter after all."

She was a pretty youngster, the same age as Jonas Fuller's girl. In fact the two were close friends. Sam McCool decided suddenly that the best thing was to tell her what was going on. He said, "That fire at Bill Clay's house—Judge Fuller and I both think the

51

Wileys started it."

"For heaven's sake, why would they do a thing like that?"

"Clay was on the jury. They were trying to intimidate him."

"Are you sure?"

He shook his head. "Not sure enough to jail anyone." He paused a moment. "I also think they threatened Susan Fuller as a way of getting to the judge."

"Pa, that's awful." Mary's face was pale.

He said, "I'm not telling you to worry you. And I don't think they'll bother you because I haven't anything to do with the way the trial comes out. But I thought you ought to know what's going on."

He could see that he had frightened her. She said, "I'll go see Susan right away."

He shook his head. "I wouldn't do that if I were you. Jonas doesn't know I suspect they've threatened her. I'd as soon he didn't know. I'd as soon he'd tell me himself— when he's ready."

She nodded. "Of course, Pa." There was compassion in her eyes. "What an awful thing—to have to decide between Susan's safety and what he knows is right. Can't you just put the Wileys all in jail?"

He shook his head. "Too many of them

for that. Besides, I'd guess only one of them made the threat. Jailing him wouldn't keep the others from going through with it.''

"What are you going to do then? What can you do?''

"I wish I knew. But right now I've got to find some men to watch the Wileys and make sure they don't try getting to the other jurors too.''

"Will you be home for supper?''

He nodded. "I'll be home at six o'clock.''

He went out, mounted his horse and rode on uptown, heading for Karl Burbach's little shack on the bank of Canyon Creek.

Karl was sitting on a wooden bench beside the door, whittling. There was a pile of shavings at his feet. He had a corncob pipe in his mouth and occasionally he let a thin puff of smoke escape his lips.

He was whittling a chain out of a tree branch. The chain was already four or five feet long and there were still several feet of branch left. He glanced up. "Hello, Sam.''

"I want you to go down to the hotel. Sit on the front porch. If Simon Wiley leaves the hotel, follow him. I want to know where he goes and what he does.''

"What if he sneaks out the back door?''

"You tell Mike Lassiter to put the padlock

on the back door for tonight. You tell him I said so."

Karl carefully laid his chain and tree branch on the bench. Without looking back, he headed toward town.

Sam McCool put his horse down into the brushy bottom and crossed Canyon Creek. He climbed out on the other side and headed for Juan Gallegos's house.

Canyon Creek had a small Mexican district. Some of the houses were built of adobe bricks, handmade by their occupants. There was a string of red chili peppers hanging from the rafter of the Gallegos porch. A number of barefooted children were playing in the narrow, dusty street.

Three dogs barked furiously at McCool's horse and the sound brought Juan to the door. McCool called, "Go down to the hotel, Juan. Sit on the porch and if Andrew Wiley comes out, follow him. I want to know where he goes and what he does."

Juan came out, settling his broad-brimmed straw hat onto his head. He headed down the narrow, dusty street in the direction of the hotel, scuffing his sandal-clad feet as he walked.

McCool stared after him. Putting men to following the Wileys wouldn't prevent threats from being made against the jurors. It would only insure that he found out. And even that wasn't going to help. Once the threats were made, the damage would be done. Still, it might discourage the Wileys and give courage to the jurors if one or more of the Wileys were arrested and charged with jury tampering.

He rode back across the creek to the house of Nate Shibell and asked him to go to the hotel and keep track of Thomas Wiley. Shibell left immediately, heading for the hotel.

Solomon's three sons, those who were in town, would be watched. That left Solomon for McCool to watch. He rode back downtown and tied his horse in front of the courthouse. He walked along the street until he came to the bank, half a block up the street from the hotel.

He found a place at the window from which he could see the front door of the hotel. He waited patiently, never taking his eyes off the door of the hotel.

Chapter 6

As the fire that had consumed the Clay home slowly died, the Wileys began to drift away. One of the smaller boys got into a fight with one of the town boys and was getting the best of it when Solomon picked him up, kicking, by one arm and held him dangling.

Solomon looked at his wife. "Take 'em home," he said. "Bring 'em back in time for court tomorrow."

She nodded, without looking at him. She spoke sharply to the others and they turned and marched down the street, between thirty and forty of them, women, children, boys that were almost grown.

Solomon and his three sons waited until they had gone. Then Solomon said, "Let's go back to the hotel."

He led the way, a shaggy patriarch, while

his sons followed a few steps behind. Solomon didn't talk and neither did his sons. He was like a shaggy old dog wolf prowling through some wilderness with his half-grown pups, teaching them, by example, how to hunt. They reached the hotel and strode inside. In single file they went upstairs and disappeared into their two adjoining rooms.

Solomon poured himself a drink, then passed the bottle to his sons. He stared at Sime. "Anybody see you set fire to that house?"

Sime shook his head. "I don't think so. I was careful. I stayed in the alleys as much as I could."

Solomon nodded. Sime asked, "What do we do now?"

"We talk to some of the other jurors."

"Won't McCool be expecting that?"

Solomon nodded. "We'll go out the back door. One at a time. Sime, you go first. Talk to Steve Carnes. Know where he lives?"

Sime nodded. Solomon said, "Get going, then."

Sime gulped what was left of his drink. He looked longingly at the bottle. His father gave him no encouragement so he went on out the door. After a few minutes he was back. "They've got the back door of the hotel locked, Pa. There's a padlock on it."

Solomon nodded. "All right, go out the front door then. But you stop over there in front of the saloon and look up here. If I wave my hat, it means there's somebody following you."

"What do I do then?"

Solomon looked at him disgustedly. "I'll tell you what not to do. Don't lead him to Steve Carnes's house. Just wander around town a while letting him follow you. After half an hour, you can come back here."

"Without seeing Carnes?"

"Without seeing Carnes. McCool ain't stupid. He knows we threatened Clay. He knows we set fire to his house."

"How we going to get to them other jurors if McCool is watching us?"

"He couldn't have more'n two or three men at the most. If we get one followin' each of you, maybe there won't be any left to follow me."

Simon went out, closing the door. A few minutes later he appeared in the street in front of the hotel. He crossed it and walked along the other side until he came to the saloon. Here he paused and glanced back toward the hotel.

As soon as he had reached the far side of

the street, Solomon had seen Karl Burbach cross. Burbach was hurrying, stowing his knife in his pocket, brushing shavings from his pants.

Solomon waved his hat. Sime turned and went on down the street, with Burbach following. Solomon said, "All right, Andrew. You're next."

Andrew went out the door, appearing shortly thereafter in the street. He crossed and went as far as the saloon. He stopped and took a moment to roll a cigarette. Lighting it, he glanced up at the hotel. Solomon waved his hat, having seen Juan Gallegos following him. He said, "All right, Tom."

Tom went out, pausing at the saloon as had the other two. Again Solomon waved his hat, and Tom went down the street with Nate Shibell shuffling along behind.

Solomon scanned the street now, looking for Sam McCool. McCool was not in sight. Cramming his hat down onto his uncut red mop of hair, Solomon went out. So big was he, that the floor creaked thunderously beneath him as he walked. He went down the stairs, pausing at the foot to look over those who were in the lobby. Satisfied that none was interested in him, he went out onto the veranda.

It was deserted, but that failed to satisfy him. He paused at the foot of the veranda steps and once more looked carefully up and down the street. McCool was not visible.

He walked slowly along the street. He paused at the saloon, turned and scanned the street again carefully. It was not deserted by any means, but no one seemed to be paying any particular attention to him.

He stepped into the saloon. He crossed to the bar, ordered and paid for a beer then carried it to the window. Once more he studied the street and found nothing suspicious about it.

He gulped the beer, carried the mug back to the bar, then went back out. He walked slowly toward the next intersection.

Nearly there, he ducked suddenly into a passageway between two buildings. It was only a foot and a half wide and it was littered with tin cans and trash. Solomon stopped, waited a moment, then peered cautiously out.

If he had expected to see a pursuer running to catch up, he was disappointed. Nothing seemed in any way different than it had before.

Finally satisfied, he turned and picked his

way along the passageway. He reached the far end, which fed into a yard littered with broken wooden boxes and tin cans. He reached the alley, walked along it until he came to the street and then turned north.

Twice he turned his head to look behind. Grinning, then, he forgot his anxiety and went single-mindedly about his task.

He headed toward Ralph Pew's house. He had selected Pew because Pew had the most to lose. Pew had five daughters ranging in age from six to seventeen. He should be susceptible to threats.

Sam McCool watched his three deputies as they lounged on the veranda of the hotel. He hoped Mike Lassiter had put a padlock on the back door of the hotel but he didn't dare absent himself from his vantage point inside the Canyon Creek Bank long enough to find out.

He had chosen the bank because the windows hadn't been washed for months. He knew that while he could see out into the sunlit street well enough it was virtually impossible for anyone more than a few feet away to see into the darkened interior of the bank.

Less than ten minutes passed. Then he saw

61

Sime Wiley come out of the hotel and cross the street. Karl Burbach followed him, stuffing his knife into his pocket and brushing shavings from his pants. Sime stopped at the saloon and glanced back toward the hotel. McCool saw someone in the hotel window wave a hat.

He grinned faintly to himself. Old Solomon was no fool. He'd guessed the sheriff would have his sons followed. Now, undoubtedly, Sime would wander aimlessly around town for a while, letting Karl follow him. And while he did, someone else would do what Solomon had sent Sime out to do.

Interestedly he watched as Andrew came out, to be followed by Juan Gallegos, to be signaled similarly by Solomon. Tom came last, followed by Nate Shibell. He also got the hat signal from the window of the hotel. McCool muttered to himself, "It's your turn, you sly old son-of-a-bitch."

He did not have long to wait. Solomon came from the hotel and slowly crossed the street to the saloon. Here he paused, turned and scanned the street. He went in and McCool knew he was watching through the window of the saloon.

Solomon was in the saloon barely long enough to gulp a beer. When he came out, he once more scanned the street.

McCool knew he was taking a chance that Solomon would give him the slip. If that happened, another juror would get threatened and there would be no way he could undo the damage once it had been done.

This was taking a chance, but if it paid off, it would pay off handsomely. If he could catch Solomon in the act of intimidating a juror, he could put him in jail for the duration of the trial. He could see to it that Solomon spent a couple of years repenting in prison at Cañon City.

Solomon ducked suddenly into a narrow passageway. McCool squinted, trying to see better. Solomon would probably peer out and study the street. If nothing aroused his suspicions, he'd go ahead and do what he had set out to do without any more delay.

McCool had gone over the jurors in his mind, one by one, trying to decide which of them Solomon was most likely to approach. Now he wasn't in much doubt. Ralph Pew had five daughters. And since the Wileys seemed to like threatening girls, he would probably be the one they picked.

He gave Solomon time to study the street. Then he left the bank, hurrying. He cut up a side street, almost running, wishing he had his horse but knowing the animal would make him too conspicuous.

Ralph Pew lived in a big two-story brown frame house two blocks off Main and only a block from the bed of Canyon Creek. At each alley, McCool stopped long enough to glance along it on the chance he might glimpse Solomon crossing farther down. But he didn't see anything.

He traveled north until he reached the alley that ran behind Ralph Pew's house. Watchfully, he trotted along it until he came to the stable behind Pew's house.

He was out of breath. He stood there in the alley panting raggedly. He had no way of knowing whether Solomon Wiley was in Pew's house or not. But if he was, it would be prima facie evidence that he was threatening the man.

When his breathing had quieted, he crouched and moved along the sagging board fence until he reached a spot just below Pew's kitchen window. He heard a deep and rumbling voice, but the window was closed and he could not make out any words. Then he heard another voice, also a man's voice but not as deep as the first had been. Again he could make out no words but the anger in the voice was unmistakable.

He stepped through the fence at a spot where a couple of boards were gone and went closer until he stood directly beneath the window. It was now obvious that two men were arguing inside.

Carefully, so as not to be heard, McCool approached the kitchen door. He turned the knob slowly and opened the door an inch or so.

He could now hear the voices plainly and could plainly hear the words. Solomon said, "Yellin' at me ain't goin' to get you nothin' but trouble, Pew. But you'd better hold out for acquittal because if you don't, there ain't no tellin' what might happen to them girls of yours. They're pretty an' some of my boys sure fancy pretty girls."

McCool kicked open the kitchen door, stepping through and drawing his gun as he did. He said sharply, "Don't move, Solomon. Ralph, get his gun."

Solomon had swung quickly around as McCool came bursting in the door. When he saw the gun, he froze. Now he said, "We was just havin' a friendly talk, McCool, wasn't we, Mr. Pew?"

McCool nodded. "Yeah. I heard it. Same kind of visit you had with Clay. You're under arrest for jury tampering.''

Solomon grinned at him. He glanced at Pew, warningly, then back to the sheriff again. ''You got to have a complaining witness an' Pew ain't goin' to say nothin'. Are you, Mr. Pew?''

Pew, pale-faced, swallowed with difficulty. McCool said, ''I don't need him. I heard you threaten him.''

Solomon did not reply. Pew had his gun and was holding it gingerly. McCool crossed the room, took it from him and stuffed it into his belt. Glancing at the doorway leading to the dining room, he saw several of Pew's daughters clustered there. All of them looked scared.

He said, ''Go on, Solomon. Down to the jail.''

Solomon went out, scowling. He didn't speak until they had gone almost half a block. Then he said, ''Better not push this, McCool. You'll be sorry if you do.''

McCool didn't answer him. Solomon Wiley might be right. But if the people of this town, and this county, were going to let the Wileys terrorize them, then it would end up no fit place for anyone. Jude Wiley had killed a girl in Canyon Creek. If he was allowed to get away with it, no woman could ever feel safe again.

Solomon Wiley had, furthermore, threatened two jurors and the judge. Unless he was punished properly for that, the judicial system in this county would henceforth be a farce.

As they crossed the courthouse lawn Solomon growled, "I want to see my boys."

"You'll see 'em soon enough."

"I ought to take that damn gun away from you and ram it down your throat." Solomon turned his shaggy head and glared threateningly at McCool.

McCool thumbed the hammer back with an audible click. "Come ahead."

Solomon chuckled humorlessly. He went into the sheriff's office and the sheriff followed him cautiously. He knew how dangerous Solomon Wiley was. He stayed far enough back so that Solomon couldn't take him by surprise.

Solomon opened the door leading to the cells. Jude's voice said, "What you doin' here, Pa?"

"Never mind." He shuffled along the stone-paved corridor.

McCool said, "Put your hands against the bars above your head. Spread your legs and spraddle out."

Solomon made no move to comply. McCool said evenly, "By God, you do what I tell you, or I'm going to put a bullet in your leg. Now move!" He meant exactly what he said.

Solomon faced the bars. He reached above his head and gripped them so hard that his knuckles turned white. He moved his legs back, spreading them.

Cautiously, McCool approached. Keeping his gun cocked and ready, he searched Solomon for weapons with his left hand. He found a bone-handled pocket knife, but nothing else. Stepping back he said, "Get inside."

Solomon complied. McCool slammed and locked the door with a distinct feeling of relief. He knew Solomon had been capable of putting up a fight. He knew there was a chance Solomon could have won it, despite the fact that he was unarmed.

Solomon repeated, "I want to see my boys."

McCool shut the door between the cells and the sheriff's office and turned the key. He took it out of the lock and dropped it into his pocket. He was sweating heavily.

He was afraid of Solomon. The man was so goddam big. And if he was afraid, he could hardly blame others in Canyon Creek for also being afraid.

Gloomily he thought that Judas Wiley was going to end up getting off. There had already been enough pressure put upon the jurors and the judge to make a conviction impossible.

Chapter 7

For several moments after Sheriff McCool had herded Solomon Wiley out of his house, Ralph Pew, his wife, and daughters stared at one another silently. Pew was white and shaking. The chin of one of the girls was quivering. The first one to speak was Pew's wife, a plump, motherly looking woman. She said, "Oh, that awful man!"

One of the girls, Martha, asked fearfully, "Will he really hurt us, Papa?"

Pew hesitated slightly before answering. Then he shook his head. "He was just trying to scare us. How can he hurt us if he is in jail?"

But he didn't believe that and he knew neither his daughters nor his wife believed it either. Solomon Wiley was dangerous. He wouldn't stay in jail forever. And even while he was in jail, his sons were free. They might be more dangerous than their father was. Mrs. Pew asked, "What are you going to do?"

He didn't know. What he did know was that he wanted off the jury if he could get off. Then he wouldn't have to decide what he should do. His family would be out of danger and he wouldn't have to do something he knew was wrong. He said, "I'm going to see the judge."

Mrs. Pew nodded approvingly. Pew put on his hat and coat and went out the door. He rounded the house and headed down the street toward Judge Fuller's house.

Jonas Fuller came to the door with a napkin in his hand. He'd been eating supper with his daughter, Susan. Pew said, "I want off that jury, Jonas. You got to get somebody else."

"They threatened you?"

Pew nodded. "The sheriff was following Solomon Wiley and he heard him threaten me. He took him down to the courthouse and put him in jail. But I still want off that jury. I got five girls to think about."

Jonas nodded. It would do no good to try and hold Pew against his will. It took only one juror, holding out for acquittal, to set

Jude Wiley free. He said, "I'll get somebody else."

Pew thanked him nervously, perhaps a little guiltily. He turned and hurried away. Going past the house of Gus Easley, half a block from his own, he heard Easley's door slam and turned his head to see Gus hurrying down the walk toward him. Easley said, "I saw McCool bring Solomon Wiley out of your house a while ago. Did Wiley threaten you?"

Pew hesitated. Then he nodded. There was no use lying to Gus about it. The whole town would know soon enough.

"Wanted you to hold out for acquittal, huh?"

Pew nodded again.

"What'd he say he'd do if you didn't agree?"

"He said he hurt my girls."

"What are you going to do?"

"I saw the judge. He let me off."

"He let Bill Clay off too. After Solomon burned his house."

"We don't know Solomon burned his house."

"Huh-uh. We don't *know*. But we're pretty damn sure, aren't we?"

"What are *you* going to do?"

"Soon's I finish supper, I'm going to round up the others. I think we ought to have a meeting and decide."

Pew nodded, then ducked his head and hurried along the street toward his house. At least, he thought, he was out of it. He wasn't on the jury any more.

But his sense of guilt remained. If Easley called a meeting of the remaining jurors and if they all asked to be excused . . . There'd be no chance of getting another jury in Canyon Creek. Jude Wiley would probably go free.

On the other hand, if the judge refused to excuse the jurors that remained—if he appointed two others to take the places vacated by Bill Clay and himself—then the outcome of the trial would be a foregone conclusion. Jude would be acquitted because the jurors were afraid of what Solomon Wiley would do if they convicted him. The threats made against Clay and Pew had, by implication, been made against all the other jurors too.

He found it hard to meet the anxious glances of his wife and daughters when he got home. He told them he had been excused and saw the relief in all of them. He had done the proper thing, he told himself. The law had no right to ask a man to risk the safety of his family.

But he knew that wasn't true. The safety of every man, woman, and child depended on the law, on making the system work. He also knew that by asking to be excused from the jury, he had helped break the system down.

His wife put his supper in front of him. He picked at it, having no appetite. He kept telling himself angrily that a man had a right to protect his family. That, at least, was true.

He felt guilty about what he had done tonight. Tomorrow his guilt would be a little less. By the time a week had passed, he would have convinced himself that what he had done was right. Because only by self-justification can humans live with the wrongs they do.

It was full dark by the time Gus Easley finished making the calls he had to make. He had called on the other nine jurors and they had agreed to meet at his house at eight o'clock.

Back at home, he paced restlessly back and forth, deliberately working up his anger over what had happened to William Clay. Damn it, he told himself, people had a right to the protection of the law. If they were going to be asked to serve on juries, the law owed them protection from the families of those who happened to be on trial. Was the law going to replace Bill Clay's house? Hell no, they weren't. Bill Clay was going to have to start over again from scratch. And he'd get no help from anyone.

At least, Clay and his family were alive. They had not been hurt. But what about the families of the jurors that were left? What about his own family? What had the law done to protect them from the Wileys? Nothing. That's what the law had done. Nothing. And the law could, apparently, do nothing. It was up to a man to protect himself.

His mind guiltily avoided the question of what the Wileys would be like once they had challenged the law and won. He refused to think about the future crimes they might commit.

His wife sat in a rocker, a lamp beside her, sewing. Occasionally she glanced up at him, worry in her eyes. She did not question him even though she knew what he was about to do was wrong.

At a little before eight, the jurors began to arrive. Steven Carnes came first. Then Marv

Knox, then Uno Garcia. The others, except for Si Pickett, came in a group, and Si arrived last a little after eight.

Easley said, "I figure we ought to decide what to do."

Si Pickett said, "The judge said we wasn't to discuss the case. Not until all the evidence was in."

"We ain't going to discuss the case. Not Jude's case, that is. What we got to discuss is whether we want to be on this damn jury at all. Solomon Wiley went to Ralph Pew's house this afternoon and told him he'd better hold out for acquittal or something was going to happen to his girls."

Uno Garcia, his accent thick, asked, "What you think we ought to do, Mr. Easley?"

"I think we ought to do what Ralph Pew done. I think we ought to ask the judge to excuse us. There's others he can get to serve."

"What others? Who's goin' to want to be on this jury when they know what Solomon Wiley tol' Mr. Pew?"

"That ain't none of our affair. We got to look out for ourselves. If we don't, nobody else is goin' to. You think the county's going to replace Bill Clay's house for him? Hell

76

no, they ain't."

Si Pickett asked, "Who's going to ask the judge? All of us?"

"No use all of us goin' over there. Three or four would do."

Pickett asked insistently, "What three or four?"

Easley said, "You and me. Marv Knox and Uno here."

"All right. Let's get it over with."

Carnes said, "We'll wait here for you. I want to know what Jonas Fuller says."

Easley nodded. "We'll be back just as soon as we can."

He went out, followed by Uno Garcia, Knox, and Pickett. Half a block away, Pickett asked, "Who's goin' to do the talking?"

Easley said, "I will." After that there was no talk. Easley and Pickett walked together. Bebind them came Knox and Garcia, hurrying to keep up.

They reached the judge's house. The four went up on the porch and Easley twisted the bell. He twisted it twice before the judge came to the door. Easley said, "We've got to see you, Judge."

Jonas held the door for them. "All right. Come in."

They went into the judge's parlor, abashed now, turning their hats around and around in their hands. Judge Fuller lighted two lamps, then faced them with the fireplace at his back. "What do you want to see me about?"

"It's this trial, Judge. We want to be excused."

Jonas Fuller's face lost its friendliness. He asked bluntly, "Why?"

Easley said, "Hell, you know why just as well as we do. Solomon Wiley has been making threats."

"Against you?"

Easley stared down at his feet. "Well, not exactly against me. But he threatened Clay and he burned his house."

"Who told you that?"

"Some things a man don't have to be told."

"There's no proof that any of the Wileys set fire to Bill Clay's house."

"There's plenty of proof that Solomon Wiley threatened Ralph. The sheriff has him in jail on a charge of jury tampering."

Jonas said, "Suppose I did let you off? Do you think I could get another jury?"

Easley growled, "That ain't *our* business."

"That's where you're wrong. It *is* your

78

business. It's your business to see that Jude Wiley's trial continues. If you find him guilty, I will see that he receives an appropriate sentence. But if he gets off because of his father's threats, how much respect do you think the Wileys are going to have for law?"

Easley growled, "They ain't got much respect for it now or they wouldn't be threatening jurors the way they are."

"Then it's up to you to see that they get some respect for it." Jonas had difficulty looking as stern as he wanted to. He had difficulty meeting the jurors' eyes. Because he had yet to resolve his own dilemma. He himself had not yet taken a stand with regard to the threats Andrew Wiley had made against Susan a week ago.

Easley said stubbornly, "We want to be excused."

"All of you?"

"All of us. The others are over at my house now."

The judge's shoulders sagged. "I'll consider it. I'll give you my decision in court tomorrow."

Easley protested, "Hell, we don't want to come to court tomorrow. We want to be excused right now."

Jonas Fuller straightened. "You're not going to be excused right now. I told you I'd give you my decision in court tomorrow. I won't give it to you a minute sooner than that."

Easley and the others edged toward the door, grumbling. Judge Fuller cautioned them, "Any of you that fails to show up is subject to fine and imprisonment. Is that clear, gentlemen?"

Easley growled, "It's clear," and shuffled out the door and across the porch. The judge closed the door and they tramped angrily down the walk.

Easley said, "The goddam stiff-necked old son-of-a-bitch!"

Uno Garcia protested, "You should not talk about the judge that way!"

"Why the hell not? He ain't no better than any of us."

"He is better. He holds an important position. He is trying to do what he knows is right. That is something we are not doing. We are doing something we know is wrong."

Easley said angrily, "Don't make out that you ain't doin' the same thing we are. You want off that jury too."

"I want off it, but I have decided I will stay on it." Uno's voice was frightened, but it was firm.

Easley muttered under his breath, "Dumb Mexican son-of-a-bitch!"

Garcia asked, "What did you say?"

"Nothin'. I didn't say nothin'."

Garcia knew that he had lied. He didn't know exactly what Easley had said, but he had a pretty good idea. He said, "I will go home now. I will see you in court tomorrow."

The others did not answer him. He turned away from them at the corner and headed toward his own small house.

Judge Fuller stood at the door, still looking out through the door glass even though the four had disappeared. A voice from the kitchen made him turn. "You're going to have to declare a mistrial, Jonas. I can't see that you've got any alternative."

Jonas swung around. John Gebhardt stood in the kitchen door. Susan was visible behind him. "Where did you come from?" Jonas asked.

"I came in the back door. Susan let me in."

"The back door?" Jonas pushed past Gebhardt and looked at his daughter's face. She flushed painfully. Jonas glanced at

Gebhardt. "How long has this been going on?"

"How long has what been going on?" Susan asked spiritedly.

Gebhardt grinned. "I come by and talk to Susan once in a while. But nothing's 'going on.'"

Jonas shrugged. "All right. Forget it." He was unaccountably upset, as much by the fact that Susan hadn't mentioned seeing Gebhardt as he was by the revelation that Gebhardt had been seeing her.

Gebhardt repeated, "You're going to have to declare a mistrial."

Jonas scowled. "Maybe. But I'm not going to do it unless it's absolutely necessary. You and I both know that Jude Wiley killed the McCracken girl. By threatening jurors, the Wileys are admitting it. No, sir. I don't have to declare a mistrial. Not yet. I haven't taken any testimony yet. The only thing that's been done is the jury selection. I've excused two jurors and I'll select two alternates tomorrow. And from now on, the jury is going to be locked up and guarded when it's not in court."

Gebhardt shrugged. Jonas turned and stormed out of the kitchen. He went upstairs and slammed the door to his room.

But he wasn't thinking about the jurors or the trial. He wasn't even thinking about Solomon Wiley, in jail for jury tampering.

He was thinking about Susan, and about John Gebhardt, who apparently knew her well enough to come in by the back door. He was thinking that he was going to lose her soon.

He'd always known it was inevitable. But that didn't make the reality any easier to face.

Chapter 8

When Jonas Fuller stepped out of the judge's chambers at a few minutes before ten, he was not at all surprised to see only seven jurors in the jury box. Jake Tipton intoned, "All rise. Court is now in session, Judge Jonas Fuller presiding. Be seated."

Once more, the Wileys had all but taken over the courtroom, occupying at least two thirds of the seats. Jonas glanced at Andrew, Thomas, and Simon, instantly angered by their triumphant smiles.

Jonas seated himself. He said, "I excused two jurors yesterday. There should therefore be ten in the jury box. Can any of you jurors shed light on their absence?"

Gus Easley got to his feet. "Have you ruled on what we talked about last night?"

"Sit down, Mr. Easley. I asked if any of

you jurors could shed light on the absence of the other three. Let's see, Mr. Carnes is one. Mr. Knox another. Francis Jones is the third. Does anybody know where they are?''

Nobody did. Jonas said, ''Court will recess for thirty minutes. Bailiff, go to their houses and find out why they are not here.''

Jake Tipton nodded and hurried out into the hall. Jonas retreated into the judge's chambers. He knew what report Jake Tipton was going to bring back. The three jurors were ill—probably in bed. At least that was the story they would tell. Actually none of them were sick, unless by that you meant they were sick with fear.

Briefly, Jonas wondered why he kept on trying to conduct this trial. Solomon, even though he was in jail, wasn't going to let him do it. He'd throw one obstacle after another in the way and if none of them worked, he would carry out the threat Andrew had made against Susan a week ago. Jonas suddenly wanted to quit, to give up, to declare a mistrial and let some other judge take over all the grief. That was what he ought to do.

Someone knocked on his door and he called, ''Come in.''

Simon Wiley stood in the doorway and Jonas said angrily, ''Get out of here! I don't want to talk to you!''

Simon came in anyway and closed the door behind him. ''I think you'll want to hear what I have to say.''

''I don't want to hear anything you have to say. Now get out of here!''

Simon remained at the door, his hand on its knob, holding it shut so that nobody else could come in. He said, ''You're going to hear what I have to say whether you want to hear it or not. I understand the prosecutor wants you to declare a mistrial. What does that mean, that Jude is going free?''

Jonas shook his head. ''No. It means he would be retried, either in this court or in another one. Probably in another one.''

Simon nodded. ''Then I don't want you to declare no mistrial, Judge.''

Jonas got to his feet, thoroughly angered now. *''You* don't want me to declare a mistrial? Just who in the devil do you think you are, anyway?''

Simon stared at him. ''Andy tells me he likes that filly of yours. Trouble is, Andy sometimes gets rough with the things he likes. I call to mind one time he found a fawn out in the brush. He just plain squeezed that fawn to death. Didn't mean to hurt the little thing neither.''

Jonas could feel his heart thumping furiously in his chest. His hands were trembling. He shouted, "Out! Get out of here!"

The door behind Simon was yanked open. Sam McCool stood there looking in. "Something the matter, Judge?"

"Get this man out of here!"

Simon said placatingly, "I'm goin'. I'm goin'. No need to get all riled up." He backed through the door and Sam McCool came in. "Jonas, what's going on?"

Jonas said furiously, "Damn him! Damn him!"

"What'd he say to you?"

"He threatened Susan."

"Want me to arrest him too?"

Jonas shook his head. "No, sir, I don't. This trial is going on."

"They can attack the verdict later in a higher court. If they can prove you were intimidated they can say you were prejudiced against them on account of it."

"They can't prove I was intimidated unless they confess to doing it."

McCool shrugged lightly. Jake Tipton came in the door behind him. He said, "They're sick in bed. All three of them."

"Has Doc Fothergill seen any of them?"

Tipton said, "He's out in the courtroom. Want me to call him in?"

Jonas nodded and Tipton retreated through the door. A few moments later he was back. Doc Fothergill was with him.

Jonas said, "Jones, Carnes, and Knox claim they're too sick to report for jury duty, Doc. Have you seen any of them?"

Fothergill shook his head. "Want me to go see them now?"

Jonas said, "No use. I guess you can't make somebody do something they don't want to do. Jake, how many alternates have we got?"

"Two. But there are maybe half a dozen that were impaneled but not selected out there in the courtroom now."

Jonas said, "McCool, don't let them get away. We'll select four of them, and use one of the alternates. Maybe we can get this thing underway after all."

McCool went back into the courtroom. Fothergill followed, and Tipton went out last. Wearily, Jonas went out into the courtroom, hearing Tipton's instant bark, "All rise."

He seated himself behind the bench. The formalities of selecting an additional four jurymen were soon over and the complete jury was seated in the jury box.

Gus Easley got to his feet again, "Judge, what about that thing we talked about last night?"

Jonas said coldly, "Sit down."

"We got a right . . ."

"Sit down!"

Sullenly, Gus Easley sat down. Jonas said, "Your request is denied. The trial will proceed." He looked at John Gebhardt. "Proceed."

Gebhardt got to his feet. "The State calls Sheriff Sam McCool."

McCool said a few words to Karl Burbach, sitting directly behind the prisoner, then came forward to the stand. Tipton said, "Raise your right hand."

McCool did, placing his other hand on the Bible in Tipton's hand. Tipton administered the oath in a singsong, the words of which ran together and were hardly distinguishable. McCool sat down.

Gebhardt said, "You were on duty the night Ruth McCracken was killed, weren't you?"

"Yes, sir."

"And you discovered her?"

"Yes, sir."

"Please tell us what happened. In your

own words.''

"Well, I'd left the courthouse. Usually I take a stroll down the street about ten or eleven o'clock.''

"Why?''

McCool looked surprised. "Just habit I guess. Nothin' much ever happens in this town.'' He grinned. "I guess a little walk before bedtime makes me sleep.''

A titter ran through the courtroom. Gebhardt said, "Tell us what happened, Sheriff.''

"Yes, sir. I was passin' the alley behind the hardware store when I heard what I reckoned was a moan. I went into the alley an' I found Ruth McCracken lyin' there.''

"Was that where she had been attacked?''

"No, sir. I don't guess it was.''

"Why do you say that?''

"Well, later I found a trail—in the alley dust—where she'd been dragged.''

"Did you follow that trail?''

"No, sir. Not all the way. It petered out. I figure Ruth was carried part of the way and dragged the rest.''

"What did you do? When you found her, I mean?''

"Well, sir, I yelled. Ruth seemed too bad hurt to just pick her up, and carry her to the doc. I yelled and when someone stuck his head in the alley and asked what was goin' on, I told him to go after Doc."

"Who was it?"

"I couldn't tell. He was scared and I didn't recognize his voice."

"Never mind. Go on."

"Well, I took off my coat and covered Ruth. I lighted a match and looked at her. I couldn't see any blood where she'd been shot, but she was pretty bad beat up and bleeding from the mouth and nose."

"Did you talk to her?"

"Not very much. I asked her how bad she was hurt. She just moaned some more."

"Did you ask her who did it to her? Who hurt her?"

"Yes, sir. I asked her. It was just after Doc arrived. I was afraid whatever he did to her might make her lose consciousness. So I asked her who hurt her."

"What did she say?"

"She said it was Jude Wiley. She said he beat her with his fists."

"Did Dr. Fothergill hear what she said?"

"Yes, sir. He heard. Later I made up a statement about what Ruth said before she died. Doc signed it. You have it."

"All right, Sheriff. Let's leave Miss

McCracken for a moment. What happened the next day?"

"Why, first thing in the morning I went out to the Wiley place. I arrested Jude Wiley and brought him in to jail."

"You arrested him? All by yourself?"

McCool looked embarrassed. "You don't have to make it sound like that. I thought about takin' a posse out. But that Wiley place is a fortress. If they wanted to defend it they could—against the whole damn Army I guess, if they were determined enough."

"All right. You went out there all by yourself. What did you find?"

"Well, I talked to Solomon. That's Jude's pa. I told him I wanted Jude. Told him what Jude had done."

"Did he give up his son? Just like that?"

"No, sir. He asked me what I'd do if he refused. I said I reckoned we'd have to come in and get him. I said I'd get a posse together and that I'd get Jude in the end, one way or another."

"And?"

"Why I guess he believed me. He called Jude, who was in another part of the house. Jude surrendered to me and I brought him in to town."

"What did Jude look like?"

"He was scared."

"No. I mean, was there anything unusual about the way he looked?"

"Oh. You mean the scratches. Sure. He had fingernail scratches all over his face."

"How do you know they were fingernail scratches?"

"They looked like it. And there was flesh under Ruth McCracken's fingernails."

"Thank you, Sheriff." Gebhardt turned to look at Norman Kissick, the defense attorney. "Cross-examine."

Kissick got to his feet. He was plainly nervous, plainly scared. If the Wileys hadn't been relying on threats to get Jude freed, Jonas thought, they'd demand another lawyer, one with more experience. Kissick cleared his throat. "Are you . . . are you sure Ruth McCracken named Jude Wiley as her attacker?"

"Yes, sir. I asked her who did it and she said Jude."

"Did she just say, 'Jude'?" There was a hopeful tone in Kissick's voice.

McCool shook his head. "No, sir. She said Jude Wiley. She said it several times."

"Couldn't you have misunderstood? You said she was moaning, and she died a couple of hours afterward."

McCool looked pityingly at him. "I didn't misunderstand. Neither did Doc Fothergill. She said Jude Wiley. Hell, man, she left the dance with him."

"With him?"

"Well, maybe not 'with him.' People I talked to said he followed her."

"Followed her?"

"You keep repeating things after me. Do you want me to speak louder?"

Kissick flushed painfully. "No. I can hear well enough. Please go on."

"Well, in a way he followed her. They were arguin' and she ran away into the darkness. Goin' home, she said. He ran after her, still arguin'."

Kissick looked as though he'd brought out the very thing he hadn't wanted to bring out. He looked confused a moment, then said, "These scratches. Couldn't they have been made some other way?"

McCool frowned. "They looked like the marks of fingernails. There was three on one cheek, two on the other. Close together, the way they'd be."

"But couldn't they have been made by, say, barbed wire?"

"No, sir. They weren't made by anything that sharp. They were wider, and not as deep as they'd be for a barbed-wire scratch."

"But you concede they might have been made by something else."

"Well, I suppose they could—if that something was just like fingernails."

A titter of laughter went through the court. Kissick said, "That will be all."

McCool glanced up at the judge. Jonas said, "You're excused."

McCool went back and took his place beside the prisoner. Jude scowled at him.

Gebhardt called Doc Fothergill, who gave substantially the same testimony the sheriff had. He was not cross-examined by Kissick and was therefore promptly excused. Judge Jonas Fuller recessed the court until two o'clock.

Chapter 9

Immediately after he adjourned the court, Jonas got to his feet. Already there was noise and confusion in the courtroom. The testimony had been damaging and all the spectators were, it seemed, speaking at once. The bailiff shouted, "All rise," which was superfluous since everybody was already standing, waiting for the crowd to thin so that they could leave.

Jonas frowned. To the bailiff he said, "I want to see McCool in my chambers. And Ralph Pew."

He turned then, went into his chambers and closed the door. A few moments later he heard a knock and called, "Come in."

Jake Tipton opened the door and ushered in Pew and McCool. He closed the door behind them. McCool asked, "Did you want to see us?''

Jonas nodded. He looked straight at Pew. ''This trial will be over soon. Probably tomorrow.''

Pew didn't say anything. Jonas said, ''I intend to bring Solomon Wiley to trial immediately afterward. I want a signed statement from you and one from McCool giving the details of Solomon's threat against your family.''

McCool said, ''Sure, Jonas. I'll write it out right now.'' He came toward Jonas to accept the paper and pen Jonas held out to him. He backed to a desk, sat down and began to write. Pew looked scared.

Jonas held out paper and pen to him. Pew said, ''I don't want to sign any statements, Judge.''

''I didn't ask you whether you wanted to or not. A felony that directly concerns this court was committed in your presence. I want a statement from you regarding it.''

Pew stared at the floor. He shuffled his feet uncomfortably, then shook his head.

''You mean you refuse?''

''Isn't the sheriff's word enough?''

''No, it's not enough. If all I have is the sheriff's statement, then it's only the sheriff's word against Solomon's. Unless you testify.''

"I don't want to testify."

"You haven't any choice. I'll subpoena you and you'll have to testify."

Pew glanced up. There was a stubborn, unyielding expression in his eyes. "You can't make me say something I don't want to say."

"Are you saying you won't testify?"

"I won't say what you want me to say."

"I can subpoena your girls and your wife. And I will. Make no mistake about that."

Pew stared steadily at him, no longer afraid, no longer even ashamed. "They'll say what I tell 'em to say, Jonas. They'll say McCool is wrong."

Jonas saw his case against Solomon evaporating. He glanced at Sam McCool helplessly. McCool had stopped writing and was staring unbelievingly at Pew.

Jonas fought the angry frustration within himself, remaining silent while he did. At last he said, "Ralph, what you're doing is wrong. Solomon Wiley has committed one of the worst crimes possible. He has attacked the very foundations upon which our laws and justice rest. If he is permitted to get away with it, he and his family will henceforth be immune from prosecution for any crimes they may commit. Do you think your daughters will be safe from his family then?''

Pew said angrily, ''I don't give a damn about the future, Judge. All I care about is right now. You're not going to make me sign any statements. You're not going to make me say anything I don't want to say.''

''We'll see about that, by God.''

''You finished with me?''

Jonas nodded. Pew went to the door, opened it and left.

Jonas stared at Sam McCool. He said disgustedly, ''You'd just as well let Solomon Wiley go.''

''You mean he's going to get away with what he did?''

''Looks that way, doesn't it?''

''I'll still testify against him.''

''Sam, it won't do any good. Pew and his wife and daughters will get on the stand and say it never happened. There isn't a jury in the county that wouldn't let him go.''

''Well, that's a hell of a goddam thing!''

Jonas nodded. ''You're right. It is.''

''The lousy yellowbelly!'' McCool said angrily.

Jonas shook his head. ''He's got five daughters, Sam. He knows Solomon will do what he threatened to.''

''But he was excused from the jury.''

Jonas nodded. "He knows the threat will carry over to Solomon Wiley's trial."

"I still say he's a gutless son-of-a-bitch."

Jonas stared at McCool's face for a moment. They were old friends and he valued McCool's esteem. He wondered what McCool would say if he knew the Wileys had threatened Susan and that he still hadn't made up his mind what he was going to do about their threat. He said, "Put yourself in Ralph Pew's shoes. Suppose it was your daughter that Solomon had threatened? What would *you* do?"

McCool stared angrily at him. "I hope, by God, I'd have the guts to stand up to him!" But there was a shadow of doubt in the way he frowned.

Jonas said, "No use writing that statement, Sam. And you'd just as well release Solomon from jail."

"I'll be damned if I will. Not until I'm ordered to."

Jonas wavered. Finally he said, "All right. Keep him overnight."

McCool got up and walked to the door. He went out, slamming it savagely after him. He stalked across the now empty courtroom and out into the hall. Damn, he thought angrily. Damn!

Jonas Fuller had disappointed him. He'd never known Jonas to be so wishy-washy. Usually Jonas was like a rock, scrupulously honest and unbending where a principle was concerned.

Susan had been threatened too, he thought. And that explained Jonas's refusal to condemn Ralph Pew's cowardice. Maybe Jonas had decided to give in to Solomon himself. Maybe that was why he refused to condemn Pew.

McCool went downstairs, feeling more helpless than ever before in his life. Jude Wiley had killed Ruth McCracken but it was beginning to look as if he was going to get away with it. The whole Wiley family was laughing at the law and there wasn't anything he could do.

But even if Jonas *had* been threatened through Susan, how could he let Jude Wiley go? There was a jury in the case, and they would decide Jude Wiley's fate.

Then he shook his head. No matter how damaging the testimony against Jude, it was still within a judge's power to instruct the jury to bring in a verdict of not guilty. And once that verdict had been brought in, Jude would be free. He could never be tried again, even though it could be proved that his family had intimidated the judge. Only in the case of a guilty verdict could the decision be appealed.

Two of Solomon Wiley's sons were waiting in his office. They stood there, big, unwashed, and unshaved and he could smell them the minute he stepped through the door. Karl Burbach, who had brought Jude back to his cell when the trial recessed, said, "They're waiting to see you, Sam."

McCool scowled at them. He said, "Take off your hats."

Sullenly they did. He snarled at them, "What the hell do you want?"

"We want to see our pa."

"Well, you can't. Not now. I've got to get meals for him and Jude before court convenes again at two. You come back tonight."

"You got no right to tell us we can't see our pa," Andrew said.

"Maybe not but I'm saying it."

Andrew said, "Come on, Sime. We'll go see the judge."

Sam McCool said, "Oh hell, go ahead. See him if you want. But you get five minutes and not a damn minute more!"

He unlocked the door leading to the cells. Andrew and Sime went through. McCool closed the door. He stood beside it, knowing how thin it was, knowing it was important that he hear what was discussed between Solomon Wiley and his sons.

Apparently they feared being overheard because what they did say was said in whispers. McCool looked at his watch. Fidgeting, he gave them exactly five minutes and not a second more. Then he yanked open the door. He heard Solomon saying, ". . . in the icehouse. That's the safest . . ." and then Solomon's voice stopped suddenly. McCool said, "Time's up."

"How about five minutes more?"

"I said your time was up. Now get the hell out of here."

Grumbling, they came along the corridor. He didn't like the way they looked at him. Neither did he like the expression on Solomon Wiley's face.

Andrew and Sime went through the office and slammed the outside door. McCool said, "I'll go down and get you two something to eat."

Solomon said, "I'll have a steak, McCool. Rare."

"You'll have what I bring back." He turned to go.

Solomon called, "Did Pew withdraw his complaint?"

McCool swung around. How could Solomon have known about that? Then he realized that Solomon's sons had probably told him about the judge summoning both Pew and him. He'd put two and two together and made a lucky guess. McCool asked, "What makes you say a thing like that?"

"Did he?"

"Nope. You'd just as well get used to the idea of spending some time in jail."

"If Pew changed his story, you'll have to let me go."

"Don't hold your breath until I do." McCool went out, closing the door behind him. To Burbach he said, "I'll get us all something to eat. Don't let anybody in there until I get back."

Burbach nodded. He was idly sharpening his knife on a pocket stone.

Glad to get away, McCool went out into the midday sun. He hurried the block and a half to the Ace-High Cafe. The special was beef pie, which he liked. He ordered four trays made up and sat down at the counter to wait. Juanita Gallegos, wife of Juan Gallegos, brought him a cup of coffee. She was a fat pleasant-faced woman with a ready smile. She was perspiring from the heat of the kitchen. "How is the trial going, Mr. McCool?" she asked.

He shrugged. She knew what the testimony of both this morning's witnesses had been. By now everybody in town knew that. She knew that he and Doc Fothergill were the only ones who had talked to Ruth McCracken before she died. But a lot of people had seen the scratches on Jude Wiley's face when he was brought in.

She said, "People are saying those Wileys are trying to scare the men who are on the jury. They are saying the Wileys burned Mr. Clay's house too."

McCool said, "People will gossip about anything."

"You mean it isn't true?"

McCool said, "One thing at a time, Juanita. Right now we're trying Jude Wiley for murder. Let's get that over first."

She studied him perplexedly, obviously disappointed at her failure to get more out of him. He said impatiently, "How about those trays? Court convenes again at two."

"I'll see if they're ready." She went into the kitchen and returned a few moments later carrying the trays, stacked four high. McCool took them and went through the door, which she held for him.

He hurried the block and a half back to the courthouse. He'd thought he was hungry, but when he sat down to eat, he just picked at his food. He couldn't get the trial off his mind, and he couldn't help wondering if the Wileys had managed to get to any of the other jurors and threaten them.

Finished, he got the trays from Solomon and Jude, then stacked all four on the table near the door. Burbach would take them back later when he got a chance. McCool looked at his watch. It was a quarter of two. He said, "Get Jude for me. Be sure and put the cuffs on him."

Burbach went back and unlocked Jude's cell. He returned a few moments later, following Jude, whose hands were cuffed in front of him. McCool said, "Let's go."

Jude looked smugly triumphant and McCool wondered what old Solomon and his sons had cooked up now.

Nothing but trouble, that was sure.

Chapter 10

Jonas Fuller sat behind his desk for a long time after McCool and Pew had left. He knew Susan was expecting him home for dinner, but even though it was after noon, he didn't move. Frowning, he considered the alternatives available to him.

There was a good chance the trial would conclude this afternoon. The only two witnesses the prosecution had were Sheriff McCool and Dr. Fothergill, and they had already testified. So far as he knew, the defense had no witnesses. The truth of the matter was, the defense had no defense. The best Kissick could manage would be to put some of the members of the Wiley family on the stand, to testify Jude had never been violent toward the other members of his family. There couldn't possibly be any character witnesses who would testify for him among the people of the community. The Wileys were too thoroughly disliked.

He got up and began to pace restlessly back and forth. He was afraid for Susan. He shuddered to think of her in the Wileys' hands. She was so fragile . . .

He felt anger mounting in him. Damn them. By their threats they were undermining the entire system of justice and order. Everything rested on the inviolability of the courts and juries. If those things were attacked, then only anarchy was left.

And the inviolability of court and jury had been attacked here in Canyon Creek. He wondered if Solomon and his sons had managed to get to any of the jurors since new ones were chosen this morning. It wouldn't surprise him if they had. But even if they had not, quite possibly the damage was already done. All the jurors knew about Bill Clay's house and about the threats made against him previously. Some of them undoubtedly knew about the threats made against Ralph Pew's family.

Perhaps, he thought, the jury would bring in a not-guilty verdict without any interference from him. The trouble was, he didn't dare take the chance. If they should happen to bring in a guilty verdict, then it would be too late for him to do anything. Susan would be at the mercy of the Wiley clan. And even if he had her guarded, he couldn't keep her guarded indefinitely. Sooner or later the Wileys would get to her.

He glanced at his watch. Already it was a quarter of one. Susan would worry about him if he didn't get home right away. He put on his hat and went out into the deserted corridor, still uncertain as to what he was going to do. How could he turn his back on a lifetime of reverence for the law? But then how could he turn his back upon his own daughter, and completely disregard her safety?

He felt tormented, torn between two impossible alternatives as he walked toward home, tall, frowning, stooped, and slightly shuffling, a man who looked today as if the weight of the world was on his back. Several people spoke to him but he did not hear and so did not reply. Once he shuddered, as if he had a chill.

He went through the front door, closing it behind him. He called, "Susan?"

He got no reply. He could smell the pleasant odor of cooking meat. He went through the house and into the kitchen, placing his hat on the dining-room table as he did.

The kitchen was empty. The table was set for two. He could now smell fresh baked bread, and the coffee that had been pushed to the back of the stove.

He went to the back door, crossed the porch and stuck his head outside. "Susan?"

There was no answer to his call. Suddenly turned uneasy, he called more loudly, "Susan? Where are you?"

Once more only silence greeted his call. He smelled something burning and returned to the kitchen immediately. Smoke was rising from a pan of potatoes, frying on the stove. He picked up the pan and carried it to the sink, burning his hand but scarcely noticing the pain. He roared, "Susan!" and his shout reverberated through the house. Only silence answered it.

He ran out the back door, along the walk to the alley. If the Wileys had taken her, there would be tracks in the alley dust. Tracks of some kind. He reached the alley and stopped, staring down at the tracks of a buckboard there. There also were the tracks of men's boots, and the tracks of saddle horses besides those of the buckboard team. The Wileys had carried out their threat. They had kidnaped Susan. Only God knew where they had taken her, but it had probably been to their ranch on Canyon Creek. And that ranch was a fortress . . .

Jonas ran back into the house once more. He took the stairs two at a time, and searched each room upstairs. He descended the stairs at a run, and similarly searched the remaining rooms downstairs.

Forgetting his hat, he ran out into the street. He was out of breath and his heart pounded furiously inside his chest. At a rapid walk, he headed toward the courthouse. If anything had happened to Susan, he thought, he would kill Solomon Wiley himself. He also would kill Jude. They might have Susan as a hostage to guarantee Jude's release. But he had two hostages to guarantee Susan's safety and eventual release.

He crossed the courthouse lawn diagonally. People were beginning to assemble for the afternoon session of the court. He yanked out his watch and looked at it, startled to see that it was half-past one. Where had the time gone, he asked himself. It must have passed more swiftly than he thought as he sat deliberating in his chambers before going home for dinner. If he'd only gone home immediately, he thought. He might have gotten there in time. Susan might still be safe.

But he didn't believe that, even as he thought it. His presence at home wouldn't have kept them from kidnaping Susan. Overpowering him would have been simple for three or four men as burly as the Wileys were.

He ran down the short flight of steps to the door of the sheriff's office and flung open the door. He confronted a startled Jude Wiley and an equally startled Sam McCool. McCool exclaimed, "Jonas! What's the matter?"

Jonas stared furiously at Jude. Jude had the audacity to grin at him. And suddenly Jonas could stand no more. He leaped at Jude, groping for his throat.

Jude brought up his hands, cuffed in front of him. His strength was twice what Jonas's was and he easily broke Jonas's grip upon his throat. He stepped back and Sam McCool stepped between the two. "Hey! What do you think you're doing? What's the matter with you anyway?"

Jonas's hands and knees were trembling. His heart was pounding. He said between clenched teeth, "The bastards took her!

They took Susan!"

"Who took her? The Wileys? How do you know?"

"Tracks. I found the tracks of a buckboard in the alley behind the house. Boot tracks too, big ones. And the tracks of a couple of saddle horses. They took her all right."

McCool put his hands on Jonas Fuller's arms. He said, "Sit down, Jonas. Sit down and cool off. Let me put Jude back into his cell. Then we can talk."

"Sit? Talk? God damn it, man, I told you they had Susan!"

McCool said soothingly, "I know how you feel. But getting excited isn't going to help. If they've got her, they've got her. They've probably taken her out to their ranch. And you know what that place is like. They could hold it against an army if they had to."

"We've got to do something!"

McCool said, "Get back into your cell, Jude."

"What about my trial?" There was studied insolence about the man.

McCool gave him a savage push. Jude stumbled and almost fell. McCool said, "I told you to get in your cell. Do it, you son-of-a-bitch!"

Startled, Jude obeyed. McCool followed him and locked him in. Returning, he closed the door separating the office from the cells. He faced Jonas, fumbling for his pipe. "Now. It's time I heard it all, don't you think?"

"They threatened Susan more than a week ago. Told her if I didn't find some way of seeing to it Jude went free, the same thing would happen to her that happened to the McCracken girl."

"Why didn't you tell me? I could have put her under guard."

"What kind of guard could you provide? One man? One man wouldn't even slow the Wileys down."

McCool said, "The trial isn't over. She's safe at least until it is."

"It will probably be over this afternoon. They want me to instruct the jury to bring in a not-guilty verdict."

McCool said, "I don't know much about the law. But suppose you did, couldn't Jude be brought to trial again?"

Jonas shook his head. "Double jeopardy. He can't be tried twice for the same crime."

"The jury will probably find him not guilty anyway. They know what happened to Bill Clay's house. They probably know about the threat against Ralph Pew's family."

"But I can't take that chance."

"Let's go talk to Solomon."

Jonas stood up. He felt drained, weak. He felt every single one of his fifty-seven years. He told himself angrily that this was no time to be feeling weak. He had to go on functioning. He had to be sharp and alert if Susan was going to be rescued from the Wiley family.

Rescued? How the hell could she be rescued? They could hold that valley ranch against a troop of cavalry. And even if it was eventually captured, he knew Susan would be dead. Or she would have disappeared.

McCool opened the door leading to the cells. Jude said, "What about the trial? It's supposed to be starting, ain't it?"

McCool said, "Shut up!" He went on until he stood in front of Solomon Wiley's cell. He said, "Your boys have got Susan Fuller, haven't they?"

Solomon came to the bars. "You wouldn't expect me to admit a thing like that, would you?"

"Why not? You're already charged with jury tampering."

Jonas stepped close to the bars. He looked straight into Solomon Wiley's eyes. He didn't weigh half what Solomon did but there was no fear in him. He said, "If you hurt her, I'll kill you. I'll kill you no matter how long it takes."

Solomon grinned at him. "Might take some doin', Judge."

"You're going to stay right here until she is released."

Solomon said, "Hell, Judge, I don't know where that girl is. She might never be found."

He was insolent and sure of himself and Jonas found himself wishing he had a gun. He could kill Solomon in cold blood, he thought, and enjoy doing it.

He stepped back from the bars. He turned and went into the sheriff's office again. McCool followed, looking puzzled, and closed the door.

Jonas was sweating heavily. He stared wildly at McCool and said, "If I'd had a gun I would have killed him. And I would have enjoyed doing it."

McCool said, "What's so wrong with that?"

Jonas shook his head. "You don't understand. The law has been my life. But back there the law suddenly meant nothing to me any more. And do you know why?

Because the law has broken down. The Wileys have trampled it and spit on it and they've gotten away with it.''

McCool shook his head. ''Not yet, they haven't. Jude still hasn't been acquitted. The trial isn't over yet.''

''Are you telling me I ought to go ahead with it?''

''You've got to.''

Jonas nodded reluctantly. The clock on the wall of the sheriff's office said it was two o'clock.

McCool asked, ''What did Susan want you to do? Did she want you to let Jude Wiley go?''

Numbly Jonas shook his head. ''But they didn't have her then.''

''I know Susan pretty well. I doubt if she feels any different now than she did before.''

Jonas didn't want to talk about it any more. He said, ''Bring Jude upstairs.''

''Sure, Jonas.''

''And have John Gebhardt come to my chambers. He's been seeing her. I guess it's his right to know what has happened to her.''

He went out, leaving the door ajar. He climbed the stairs. The corridor in front of the courtroom was jammed with chattering spectators. He went into his chambers and closed the door.

It was almost ten minutes before John Gebhardt knocked and came in. Jonas said, "I don't suppose you knew, but the Wileys threatened Susan about a week ago. Said I was to let Jude off or Susan would be killed the same way Ruth McCracken was."

Gebhardt's face was shocked but he didn't say anything.

Jonas said, "They've carried out part of their threat. They've kidnaped her."

Gebhardt's face was almost gray and suddenly Jonas felt a strange kind of kinship with the man. They both loved Susan, he thought.

Gebhardt asked, "Where have they taken her?"

"Out to their ranch, I suppose."

"What are you going to do?"

Jonas shook his head. "I haven't decided yet."

"You can't take any chances with Susan's life. You're going to have to instruct the jury to let Jude off."

Jonas said, "I don't know."

Gebhardt's eyes flashed. "What the hell do you mean, you don't know? You're talking about Susan. Your own daughter, Susan!"

Jonas said, "I have loved her a long time, John. A lot longer than you have, you know."

Gebhardt's shoulders slumped. He said, "I'm sorry, sir."

Jonas got heavily to his feet. "Let's go."

"Do you know what you're going to do?"

Jonas shook his head. He opened the door and stepped into the courtroom. He sat down heavily behind the bench.

Chapter II

Susan Fuller always prepared a big meal for her father at noon because he was so gaunt and thin. But no matter how much she put in front of him, he only ate sparingly, which was, perhaps, the reason he never put on any weight.

She kept trying, though, the way women have for a thousand years, to tempt his appetite.

Today was no exception to the rule. She had baked a pot roast, fresh bread, and she had potatoes frying on the stove. He would be here soon, she thought, as she turned the frying potatoes with a spatula.

She heard the sound of a buckboard in the alley and went to the back door to see who it was. She reached the door at the same time Simon Wiley did, too late to lock it and keep him from entering.

He yanked it open, grinning, and she turned and ran. She had time to regret the fact that she had stopped locking the doors before she reached the parlor and saw that the front door was open too. Andrew Wiley stood framed in it. He was grinning the same way Simon was.

Panic touched Susan. She whirled and started up the stairs but Simon, who had pursued her through the kitchen, tackled her around the ankles and brought her down.

She heard Andrew's voice, "Throw somethin' over her head. Quick, before she starts yellin'."

She was kicking, and clawing too, but it did no good. Simon held on while Andrew brought him a knitted coverlet that lay over the sofa in the living room. Simon threw it over her head and picked her up bodily.

Until now, she had been too startled to really be afraid. Now that action was impossible, terror hit her, engulfing her like a gray coldness that began in her heart and spread until every part of her was chilled. She began to shiver uncontrollably. Simon carried her, still struggling uselessly, through the kitchen and out the back door. Somewhere he had found a rope and he tied her ankles with it and her wrists, winding the rest around and around her to hold the coverlet in place. She could breathe because the coverlet was porous but her cries for help were muffled and probably didn't carry far. Once he had trussed her up like a calf, Simon threw her roughly into the back of the buckboard and spread a tarpaulin over her.

She continued struggling until Simon said harshly, "Lie still, damn you, unless you want me to rap you on the head."

After that, she stopped struggling. She knew it was no use. The Wileys probably wouldn't drive through town anyway, and even if they did, it was doubtful if any of the townspeople would interfere with them.

At least, they didn't intend to kill her immediately, she thought, or they'd have done it back at the house. They didn't intend to kill her yet because the trial wasn't over with. They were kidnaping her to make sure her father did what he had been ordered to.

And he would, now, she thought. He wouldn't hesitate a moment when he found out she was gone.

Anger temporarily drove away the chill that had crept over her. Damn them! she thought. Damn them anyway! By using her as a hostage, they would get Jude, who had most certainly bludgeoned Ruth McCracken to death, acquitted. He would go free. And sooner or later he would kill some other girl.

Simon and Andrew drove the buckboard fast, keeping the horses, for the most part, at a steady lope. The road was rough and the bed of the buckboard hard. She bounced up into the air every time they hit a bump, and came down again against those hard floor boards. Before they had gone a mile she felt as if she had been beaten. Every part of her was sore. And the ordeal had just begun.

After two miles, she became almost numb. Her consciousness began to fade. She laid as still as she could, forcing her muscles to relax because she knew it would be easier for her if she did not keep her muscles tense.

The sun beat down upon the tarpaulin that covered her. It grew hot and stifling beneath it until she thought she couldn't breathe. She laid so still that Simon said, "Take a look at her. Maybe we've smothered her."

Hands threw the tarpaulin back. After a moment she heard Andrew's voice, "She's all right. She's breathin'." But he did not replace the tarpaulin over her head again, probably because they were, by now, well away from town.

She could breathe again, but the ordeal

went on and on. She could smell the sweating team, and she could smell Andrew and Simon on the buckboard seat. Dust filtered through the coverlet with the pungent smell of sagebrush. They were taking her out to their ranch, she thought. To that valley ranch her father had said was so impregnable. They'd hold her there until her father either did what they told him to or until they decided to dispose of her.

She was under no illusions as to whether or not they'd carry out their threats. The Wileys were capable of anything. The killing of Ruth McCracken had been the first crime one of them had committed in Canyon Creek, but that didn't mean they weren't guilty of crimes committed elsewhere. Rumor said that men were buried in unmarked graves up there in the valley of Canyon Creek—Mormons who had trailed their stolen cattle there. There were also stories of Ute women raped and sometimes killed in the reservation fifty miles to the south, though nothing had as yet been proved against any of Solomon Wiley's sons.

She could hear the rushing sound made by the creek and she knew they were in the narrow canyon that led into the Wiley ranch. Sounds echoed back from the canyon walls.

Ten minutes after entering it, she heard a distant shout and an answering shout from Andrew. She supposed they had just passed the canyon guard.

Twenty minutes later, the buckboard drew to a halt. Hands dragged her out of the buckboard and dumped her roughly on the ground. She was rolled over and over as the ropes were taken off. Her hands were untied and so were her feet. The coverlet was yanked from over her head.

She stood in the barren, dusty yard of the Wiley place, surrounded by ramshackle buildings built with no discernible plan, and by chickens, shoats, and dogs of every size and breed. She struggled to her feet and limped to the buckboard. She held onto it to steady herself and to keep from falling down. A boy of perhaps fourteen stared at her with awed eyes. "What you goin' to do with her, Andy? You goin' to marry her?"

"Hell, no. She's too skinny for me. You take her an' lock her up in the icehouse, Dan, an' stand guard outside. Don't you leave it for anything. You understand?"

Dan Wiley nodded. Susan made no move. Dan said, "You come on, you hear?"

She didn't move. Dan looked at Sime and at Andrew puzzledly. "What do I got to do to get her there? Should I drag her or carry her?''

Both of the big men laughed. ''Le's see you carry her.''

Dan approached cautiously. Susan was tempted to kick him, to put up a fight, but she knew she could only lose. Besides, there was no point in antagonizing Dan. Nor was there any point in getting herself beaten because she fought. She said wearily, ''Never mind. I'll go with you.''

Andrew said, ''Now you're usin' sense. Let's hope your pa shows as much sense as you. Because if he don't . . . well, you ain't goin' to like what we do to you.''

Dan asked, ''What you fixin' to do to her?''

Both Andrew and Simon laughed again. But neither man replied.

Dan said, ''Come on,'' and Susan followed him. The ground outside each back door was white with soapsuds thrown off the stoop. Here and there a few pigs rooted for bits of garbage that had been in the dishwater, or a chicken scratched. Nobody seemed to be around. Susan supposed the whole unsavory tribe was in Canyon Creek attending Jude Wiley's trial.

Surely, she thought, Andrew and Simon

126

would be missed at the trial. And when she was also missed, both her father and Sam McCool would know who had kidnaped her.

But even if they did, what could they do? There was at least one guard on the canyon road. She remembered her father saying that besides the road there was a narrow trail into the Wileys' valley at its upper end. She supposed that was guarded too.

Every step she took hurt, so battered was she from the buckboard ride. Her wrists and ankles both were raw from chafing by the ropes.

The icehouse was a small, log building, half-sunken into a hillside. The logs were chinked with mud, and the roof was made of dirt out of which a profusion of weeds and grass had grown. The weeds were dead now, and drying, and so was the grass. Dan Wiley opened the door for her.

He was a big young man, already nearly six feet tall. He was rangy and muscular, the natural consequence of the hard work he did day in and day out. He had a fuzzy growth of whiskers on his face, and his hair was long, lying in dirty untidy curls on his unwashed neck.

Susan looked into the icehouse with dismay. There was nothing in it, no furniture, no blankets, nothing but damp sawdust and, perhaps, a few chunks of ice buried deep in the sawdust somewhere. She said angrily, "What am I supposed to do, just sit in the sawdust all the time?"

"Maybe they're fixin' to bring you a chair."

"I'll bet they are!"

He said, "You got to go in. They told me to put you in the icehouse, ma'am."

"What if I won't go in?"

He looked embarrassed. "Then I reckon I'd have to make you go in."

She didn't want a wrestling match with Dan Wiley or with anybody else right now. And she was practical enough to know that she'd end up in the icehouse no matter what she did.

Wearily she stepped in through the door. Dan closed it behind her. She had noticed a padlock hasp on the outside of the door with a forked stick in it. She heard the stick replaced, effectively locking the door at least as far as she was concerned.

The only light came through the cracks between the boards of the door, and that wasn't very much. She sank into the sawdust, which she found to be surprisingly comfortable. She scooped out a place to fit her body and laid back. She closed her eyes.

By now, she thought, her father must know she had been kidnaped. John Gebhardt also knew. So did Sam McCool. She tried to picture in her mind the three of them together.

Her father would be furious but he also would be scared. Gebhardt would be frantic. At least she hoped he would. McCool would be the calm one, the practical one. He was probably telling her father that he had no choice, that he would have to do as the Wileys demanded. He would have to see to it that Jude Wiley got off.

But could her father so compromise his principles? She honestly didn't know. What did an honorable man do when the price of his honor was the death of a dearly loved member of his family?

Why couldn't Sam McCool take hostages from among the Wiley clan? she asked herself. He already had Jude and Solomon in jail. Why didn't he take more hostages from among the Wiley women, perhaps even some of the children too? Then he could demand her release as a condition of their release?

She knew the answer to that immediately. Her father and Sam McCool were not lawless blackmailers and kidnapers. The

Wileys also knew this. So whatever threats her father and McCool made would be empty ones that the Wileys would not believe. In contrast, the Wileys' threats had to be believed.

She closed her eyes. Her body ached mercilessly. Her wrists and ankles burned and her head had begun to ache.

Somehow, she would have to get away. She would have to get a horse and make her way back to town. Perhaps when they brought her supper, she thought to herself. And then her head was reeling. She felt as though she were falling into a pit. She fell into a state that was as much uncon-sciousness as sleep. And she did not awake until Dan Wiley opened the door to tell her that her food was there.

Chapter 12

Judge Jonas Fuller sat behind his bench, looking out over it at the courtroom crowd. The Wiley family still occupied about two thirds of the seats. Solomon was, of course, missing. He was in jail. Two of his sons, who had been in court this morning, were missing too. Andrew and Simon. They must be the two who had taken Susan, Jonas thought.

John Gebhardt sat at the prosecutor's table. Jude Wiley sat beside Norman Kissick at the defense table across the aisle. Jonas reached for his gavel to call the court to order. He lifted it and brought it down thunderously on the bench.

Instantly, there was silence in the court. The startled spectators stared at him.

He had meant to call the court to order,

and to proceed with Jude Wiley's trial. But he found that he could not. He couldn't sit here conducting court as if nothing was amiss all afternoon. Not while Susan was a prisoner of the Wiley family. Not while nothing was being done to bring about her release.

He said, "This court will adjourn until ten o'clock tomorrow morning." He offered no explanation as to his reason for adjourning court. He didn't have to. The Wileys would know his reason for doing so. Soon the prominent members of the community would also know. He intended to call a town meeting immediately.

Before anyone could move, he said, "The jury will remain. So will the county attorney, Mr. and Mrs. McCracken, and William Clay." He named a dozen others who were present in the courtroom, asking them also to remain. Then he waited, while the courtroom cleared.

When it had, except for those he had asked to stay, he said, "Bailiff, close the doors and lock them. I don't want to be interrupted by anyone."

Jake Tipton closed and locked the courtroom doors. Many of those present were looking puzzled and perhaps a little scared.

McCool had sent Jude Wiley back to the cell with Karl Burbach, and had instructed Burbach to remain in the jail until he was relieved. Now Jonas looked at McCool. "Take over, will you, Sam?"

McCool said, "There have been persistent efforts to influence this trial by intimidation. As most of you know, William Clay was threatened and his house was burned. Ralph Pew was threatened by Solomon Wiley and Solomon Wiley is in jail, awaiting trial on a charge of jury tampering. But today, an even worse thing has happened. Susan Fuller, the judge's daughter, who was threatened by Andrew Wiley a week ago, has disappeared. The judge found the tracks of a buckboard in the alley behind his house. It can only be assumed that the Wileys have kidnaped her."

For an instant, there was a shocked silence in the courtroom. Gebhardt looked at Jonas, as though reproaching him for letting Jude Wiley's jury hear what he just had said.

Jonas said, "I know what I'm doing, John. The members of the jury are fully aware of what is going on. They knew Clay was threatened and they knew his house was burned. They knew about the threats made against Ralph Pew. They are entitled to know about this latest attempt to intimidate them and to intimidate me."

Doc Fothergill got to his feet. "Do you think Susan has been hurt?"

Jonas shook his head. "I doubt it. She may have been roughed up a bit, and she may have had her hands and feet tied. But they won't hurt her unless this court finds Jude Wiley guilty and sentences him to hang."

Len McCracken, the dead girl's father, asked, with considerable compassion in his voice, "What are you going to do?"

Jonas got no opportunity to reply. Anthony Lambert, mayor of Canyon Creek and owner of the lumber yard, said angrily, "I can tell you what we ought to do. We ought to go on with the trial. We ought to find Jude Wiley guilty and sentence him to hang! If we let those unwashed bullies get Jude Wiley off, then we'd just as well abandon Canyon Creek. Because life won't be worth living here!"

A chorus of angry voices agreed with him. McCool calmed them and said, "That doesn't help Susan Fuller, gentlemen."

"If they hurt her, we ought to string 'em up!"

McCool said, "That won't help her either."

Someone in the back of the room called, "Why can't we take some of the Wileys as hostages? Why can't we hold them until they let Susan go?"

"Yeah. Why can't we do that?"

Jonas said: "Because we know and the Wileys know that we wouldn't do anything to those hostages. Just because the Wileys are without principles doesn't mean that we are too."

"Then what do you suggest?"

Jonas didn't know what to suggest. McCool shouted over the pandemonium in the courtroom, "I'm going to form a posse and go out to the Wiley place!"

"What good is that? That place is a fortress and you know it is. Two men in those rocks above the road could hold an army back."

McCool shouted the objections down. "Who will volunteer? I want about a dozen men."

There was a sudden silence in the room. McCool scowled angrily. "Come on, come on. I want a dozen volunteers. Where are all the ones who were talking tough a couple of minutes ago?"

The silence held, and nobody raised his hand. At last, Len McCracken got to his

135

feet. "I'll go with you."

"Who else? Come on now, who else?"

Nobody stood up. McCool looked at Jonas helplessly. Lambert yelled, "It's no good trying to get Susan back! What we ought to do is show them they can't scare us. We ought to go on with this trial. Jude Wiley should be found guilty and sentenced to hang. If they know their threats aren't doing any good, they'll stop making them."

A chorus of voices agreed with him. Jonas stared sourly at the crowd. He fixed his glance on Lambert. "Suppose it was your daughter they were holding, Anthony? Would you still be saying that?"

Lambert couldn't meet his eyes. He stared steadily at the floor and did not reply.

McCool yelled, "With a posse of a dozen men, we can take that ranch!"

"And have old Wiley's sons coming in behind us on the road? We'd be caught like rats in a trap. We wouldn't be able to go on in or come back out."

Doc Fothergill interjected: "And Susan's life would be in jeopardy. You don't seriously think, do you, that they'd let us find her there? Even supposing we could get in?"

Sam McCool shrugged helplessly, by his

response admitting that he recognized the danger to Susan in trying to storm the Wiley place. But he was also acknowledging his failure to raise a posse from among these men. He turned his head and looked at the judge. He shrugged almost imperceptibly.

Jonas said wearily, "All right. The meeting is adjourned. Jake, take the jury to the hotel and see that nobody talks to them."

Tipton unlocked the courtroom doors. He took the jury out first. The rest of the crowd followed, leaving Jonas and Sam McCool alone. Jonas stared at the sheriff helplessly. "They've got us, Sam. They know there's not a damn thing we can do."

"You're not going to let Jude Wiley go?"

"What else can I do? They mean it, Sam. They'll kill Susan if I don't let him go."

"Maybe they're bluffing. I've still got Solomon in jail."

"They're not bluffing. You and I both know that."

"They wouldn't dare . . ."

Jonas shook his head. "They'd dare. We'd never find any trace of her. We'd never even be able to prove they'd kidnaped her."

McCool nodded reluctantly. "I suppose

you're right." His face reddened with angry frustration. "But I hate to think they're going to get away with it!"

Jonas got up wearily. McCool asked, "What are you going to do?"

"Go home and think."

Jonas followed McCool out of the courtroom, locking the door behind him. McCool went downstairs to the jail. Jonas cut diagonally across the lawn and headed home.

The stove was cold, having burned itself out during the afternoon. The pot roast was dry, but it wasn't burned. The fresh bread, in the warming oven, was still a little warm. Its aroma reminded Jonas that he hadn't had anything to eat since breakfast.

He got a knife and cut several slices of bread. He buttered them, then poured some milk and a cup of lukewarm coffee. He sat down at the kitchen table half ashamed to eat while Susan was being held prisoner. He knew it was silly but he couldn't help feeling guilty.

He finished the bread and milk and felt better because of it. He got up and once more went into the alley to look at the tracks. They had been almost obliterated by various wagons that had been down the alley during the afternoon. The ice wagon was one, he supposed. The vegetable wagon might be another one. And Marvin Levy's junk wagon might easily be a third. Besides that, wind had stirred the deep dust and blurred the tracks. If he'd had any idea of getting the sheriff and a tracker over here, he could forget it now. There wasn't enough left for the most expert tracker to be positive about.

He returned to the house. There was no need for a tracker anyway. He knew where Susan was. The trick was getting her out of there without endangering her life.

Try as he would, he could only come up with one solution. That was to give in to their demands. He'd have to see to it that Jude Wiley got off. Only that would save Susan's life.

The house seemed empty with Susan gone. He sat down and closed his eyes, remembering her, her face, her steady, honest eyes. She had been aghast at the thought that he might give in to Andrew Wiley's threat. She hadn't been afraid. Or had she? He felt his eyes burning. Hell, yes, she'd been afraid. But she hadn't let it show. She'd been firm, and strong, and she'd insisted he do what he knew was right, no matter what the consequences might be.

Once more he got up and began to pace back and forth. The hours passed with agonizing slowness as he wrestled endlessly with a problem that had no solution he could accept.

Sam McCool and his daughter Mary arrived at five thirty. Jonas let them in. McCool said, "Mary insisted on coming over and fixing your supper for you. I just tagged along."

Jonas thanked Mary, knowing why McCool had "tagged along." He was terrified for Mary. As soon as she had disappeared into the kitchen, Jonas said, "You keep her with you all day tomorrow. Or with somebody you can trust."

"I intend to."

"I appreciate your coming over. An empty house is pretty hard."

McCool said, "Jonas, we've known each other for a long, long time. Our girls grew up together. Our wives were friends."

Jonas nodded, wondering what McCool was getting at. McCool said, "I'm going to stick with you. And we're going to get Susan out. Even if we get no help from anybody else."

Jonas smiled. "You almost make me

believe we can."

McCool said, "We can. And we will. Because I can kill Solomon Wiley in his cell. If that's what it takes, I can shoot him down like I would a rabid dog."

Chapter 13

Jonas Fuller was sorry to see Sam McCool and Mary leave. The meal had been good, and both Sam and Mary had tried hard to make Jonas forget, for a little while, that Susan was in the Wiley family's hands. Their efforts failed, but just having had them try had made Jonas's torment easier.

Mary had done the dishes, so there was nothing left for Jonas to do. He climbed the stairs wearily. He looked into Susan's room and as he did his eyes burned and his throat felt tight. If he got her safely back, he told himself, he would encourage her friendship with John Gebhardt, if she wanted him. Or with any other young man she chose. It wasn't right to keep her here, taking care of him. He could hire a housekeeper easily enough. Susan was entitled to have a life of her own, a family of her own. Besides, there would be compensations for him. There would be grandchildren.

He laid his clothes over the back of a chair and blew out the lamp. He got into bed. He laid on his back in the darkness, staring at the ceiling, and his mind went back across the years, remembering Susan's mother, remembering Susan as a child. If they hurt her, he thought, he'd spend the rest of his life seeing that they paid for it, by lawful means or if that didn't work, by other means.

But vengeance wouldn't bring her back if they killed her. He must make sure nothing happened to avenge.

How? He was back to that again. By letting Jude go free? Susan wouldn't want Jude going free. She had known Ruth McCracken. She had kept Andrew Wiley's threat to herself a long time because she didn't want him to be influenced. He imagined what it must have been like for her, terrified of Andrew and his brothers, asking no help in her fear from anyone.

No. Susan would want him to do his duty fearlessly. She would be willing to accept the consequences, whatever they might be. The trouble was, he wasn't willing to let her accept those consequences.

Alternatives. What were the alternatives? He had Jude and Solomon Wiley in jail. Perhaps he could convince the other Wileys that he would exact vengeance against Solomon if Susan was hurt in any way.

He went over and over it in his mind. He knew he wouldn't be able to kill Solomon in cold blood even if Solomon's family killed Susan. It wasn't in him to murder anyone. But did they know that? Wasn't it possible he could convince them otherwise? And if they believed he was capable of killing Solomon it wouldn't matter whether he really was or not.

He'd go out there first thing in the morning, he decided finally. He'd saddle a horse and ride out there and he'd convince them that Solomon's life would be forfeited if harm came to Susan while she was in their hands.

He dozed fitfully throughout the night, dreaming often that Susan was dead, waking each time to find himself soaked with sweat. He got up finally a half hour before dawn, and dressed. He went downstairs and built up the fire sufficiently to heat the coffeepot.

He couldn't eat. But he drank two cups of scalding coffee and felt better afterward. It was gray dawn when he trudged out to the stable in back of the house and saddled up the buggy horse. He climbed stiffly to the saddle and headed out of town along the road that paralleled Canyon Creek.

He was groggy and lightheaded, probably because he had slept so little the night before. He felt a gray foreboding, as if he knew he was going to fail. But he told himself he didn't dare to fail because this was his only chance. Unless he could persuade those who were holding Susan of their father's peril, then he was doomed to fail.

He hadn't ridden a horse for years and the insides of his thighs were chafed and sore before he had gone a mile. Nor had he brought a gun. He was defenseless and unarmed, his only bargaining power the fact that Solomon Wiley was in the county jail.

Canyon Creek rose steadily after it left the town. Its bed was choked with brush and lined with willows and cottonwoods. The road crossed and recrossed it half a dozen times on bridges built of logs and covered with three-inch rough-sawed planks. The hoofs of Jonas's horse sounded hollow trotting across each bridge.

At first, the valley was wide, a mile or

more, and flat. It was covered with sagebrush and cut here and there with dry washes made by the flash floods that plagued the country in the summertime. Sometimes the road would bridge a wash. Sometimes it would simply dip into it and climb out on the other side.

The hillsides themselves were covered with scrub cedars and piñon pine. Higher, above the slide and above the rim, Jonas could see the brooding dark green of spruce interspersed with the gold of frost-touched quaking aspen trees.

Five miles from town, the canyon began to narrow down. The rims pinched in and the slides below the rims disappeared. From road to mountaintop, it was more than two thousand feet, three quarters of that straight up and down. The lower five hundred feet was a jumble of boulders, some bigger than a two-story house, these having broken off the towering rims thousands of years before and come crashing down almost to the valley floor. In these rocks an army of men could hide. Someone entering the canyon on the road would never know from behind which one the fatal shots would come. But you couldn't enter the canyon any way except by the narrow road.

At the Wiley boundary, a barbed-wire fence crossed the road. There was a wire gate here, upon which a weathered sign hung. The sign said NO TRESPASSING. PRIVATE PROPERTY.

Jonas got stiffly down from his horse. He opened the wire gate and laid it aside on the ground. He led his horse through, then replaced the wire gate. He mounted again and rode watchfully along the road.

It was dusty here, and rocky. A dozen yards to one side the creek tumbled down over the jumble of ragged rocks. Spray rose into the air, cooling it. And now the sun touched the high rims on the western side of the canyon, turning them a rosy gold.

He had gone no more than half a mile when something struck the road about a dozen feet ahead of him. Dust geysered from the spot, and moments later the report came down from above, flat and wicked and dangerous.

Jonas halted immediately, holding the prancing horse as still as possible, while the echoes and re-echoes of the report bounced back and forth from one canyon wall to the other one.

A second geyser of dust spurted from the road in back of him and again the report echoed and re-echoed back and forth until it finally died away. Jonas felt anger rising in him. The second shot had been unnecessary. They were just letting him know how helpless he was, like a cat playing with a mouse.

He heard a voice, again echoing and re-echoing until the words were made difficult to understand, "Go . . . back . . . ! The next bullet isn't goin' to miss!"

Jonas raised his head and looked around. He couldn't see the guard, indeed had no idea where the voice was coming from. He shouted, "No! I'm Judge Fuller! I want to see my daughter!"

There was an instant's silence. Then Jonas heard laughing, loud and mocking. Because of the way it echoed, sounding like the laughing of demons in the rock wilderness of hell. He waited, helplessly furious, unable to do anything but sit here and take whatever that guard up there handed out.

Again the voice came down as the laughter stopped, "Get out of here! We'll talk to you when Jude is free!"

"No! I'm not . . ." His voice echoed, ". . . not, not, not . . ."

The rifle spat wickedly, and this time the bullet struck a rock no more than half a dozen feet from the head of Jonas's horse. The animal jumped, almost unseating him. He held the reins inflexibly and the horse, which had never bucked in his life so far as Jonas knew, now began to do just that.

Jonas was thrown clear on the second jump and struck the road with a thump that knocked all the air out of his lungs. He landed on a fist-sized rock and for a moment he thought his back had been broken by the fall. He lay there helplessly, unable to move, able only to gasp and choke as he tried to suck air into his starving lungs. He didn't hear the laughing from above. He didn't hear the clatter of his horse's hoofs as the animal turned and streaked down the road.

But he heard the shots, those that stopped his horse's flight and turned him back as bullets struck the road in front of him. The horse came trotting back, halted a dozen feet short of where Jonas lay and stood there trembling.

Jonas, cruelly bruised and covered with dust, rolled and came to his hands and knees. He was too damned old for this kind of thing, he thought angrily.

But it wasn't the hurts that bothered him the most. It was the indignity. It was the mocking laughter coming from above, the way they had humiliated him and made him look ridiculous.

And he admitted something suddenly that he'd refused to admit before. This confrontation like the one in town was a confrontation between the forces of law and those of lawlessness. The challenge the Wileys had laid down was a deadly one. It was the age-old confrontation between good and evil, between God and the Devil, between the worst that is in man and the best.

He didn't dare give in. He didn't dare let either Jude or Solomon go free. If he did, the Wileys would make the existence of the people in Canyon Creek a living hell, a constant humiliation. Having compromised with right and justice once, they would be forced to compromise again and again until there was nothing left of their human dignity.

Jonas made it to his feet. From above the mocking laughter still came, but it stopped long enough for the man to yell, "Get back to town, old man! And by God, you'd better see that Jude goes free. If you want to see that pretty little girl again!" the last word echoed back and forth, ". . . again . again . . . again!"

Jonas spoke soothingly to his horse. He was trembling from head to foot. He was more furiously angry than ever before in his life. He wondered for an instant whether, if he had a gun right now and if his tormentor stood in front of him, he could shoot him down.

It was immaterial. He had no gun and his tormentor was safely up in that jumble of barren rock. He could see how impossible it would be for men to enter this canyon and take the Wiley place by force. No horse could climb into those rocks. Men on foot would be mercilessly exposed to rifle fire from above while unable to see the defenders in order to fire back.

Jonas reached his horse and seized the bridle just as the animal broke away. He was dragged a dozen feet, but he refused to release his grip. The horse finally stopped and stood, eyes rolling, ears laid back.

Again Jonas spoke soothingly to him. Slowly the horse quieted. Slowly his trembling grew less. When he judged that it was safe, Jonas put a foot into the stirrup and swung astride.

The horse pranced and jumped a couple of times but he did not buck again. Once more the harsh laugh came down from above, "I ought to make him buck you off again! By God, that was somethin' to see!''

Jonas did not look up. He rode the horse down the canyon road at a walk, looking straight ahead, trying to maintain what little dignity he had left. He had lost his hat. His clothes were torn and covered with dust. His back felt as if it had been broken from the rock he'd fallen on.

He was briefly glad Susan had not been present to see him humiliated this way. He was glad none of the people in Canyon Creek had seen.

He reached the wire gate and dismounted stiffly and painfully to open it. The sun was now well up in the sky. He supposed it was around eight o'clock but he didn't bother to take out his watch and look at it. He led his horse through, then closed the gate again, which seemed so ridiculous in the face of his fury that he smiled grimly at the contradiction.

Mounting again made every muscle in his body hurt, but he managed it. And now he lifted the horse to a jogging trot, which was the most painful gait he could have found. He wanted to get back to town well before the crowd began to form in front of the courthouse. He wanted to get home, and make himself presentable before he was seen.

He came into town around nine o'clock, staying in the creek bottom insofar as that was possible. He refused to ride down alleys, but he rode along the quieter of the streets and finally reached his home, he thought without being seen.

He stabled the horse and removed the saddle and bridle. He gave the horse a can of oats and a couple of forks of hay.

He went quickly into the house, washed and shaved in cold water and dressed meticulously. At nine thirty, he left the house and headed down the street toward the courthouse.

His muscles still hurt but nobody would have guessed it from looking at him. Ramrod stiff, he stalked along the street. His eyes were narrowed, angry, and hard. His jaw was set.

The Wileys had attacked him with the weapons they were familiar with. But Jonas Fuller had his weapons too. And today he would use them all.

Chapter 14

At ten o'clock, Jonas Fuller stepped out of his chambers and crossed to the bench. Jake Tipton intoned, "All rise," and there was a stir in the courtroom as the spectators rose. Tipton said, "Court is now in session. Judge Jonas Fuller presiding. Be seated."

Jonas stared at the crowd from behind the bench. Anger lingered in him and it showed—in the stiffness of his back, in the set of his head, in the way his glance swept the courtroom. He said coldly, "The trial of Judas Wiley will proceed." He turned the direction of his glance and let it rest on the members of the Wiley family. He said, "There have been numerous attempts to disrupt this trial and influence it. I have verified the fact that my daughter has been kidnaped and is in the hands of members of the Wiley family. I rode out there this morning and was unable to get past the guard they have stationed in the rocks overlooking the road."

The defense attorney, Norman Kissick, got nervously to his feet. He said, "I move for a mistrial. The jury has been prejudiced by remarks made from the bench."

Jonas looked coldly at him. "Sit down, Mr. Kissick. The jury was influenced by attempted intimidation long before it was influenced by me." He stared at Solomon Wiley's sons. "I would like to advise the family of the defendant that if anything else happens either to disrupt or influence this trial, the perpetrators will be arrested and jailed." He stared, frowning, for a moment more. Then, in a lowered voice, he said, "I would further like to advise the family of the defendant that Solomon Wiley is in jail along with the defendant. I make a solemn promise to Solomon Wiley's family. If anything happens to my daughter, or if she should not be recovered safely, I will personally go to the jail and shoot both Judas and Solomon Wiley in cold blood. Do I make myself perfectly clear?"

Kissick leaped to his feet again. "Your honor, those remarks are prejudicial and improper and I move they be stricken from the record. I also move once again for a mistrial."

"Motion denied. You may proceed with your defense."

Kissick looked at Jonas helplessly. "I call the defendant."

Jude Wiley got to his feet. He was tall and powerful, but he was as awkward as a half-grown bear. Even though facilities for keeping clean had been available to him, he had not made use of them. His hair was rumpled and uncombed. He had not shaved for at least a week. His clothes were dirty. Accompanied by the sheriff, he shuffled to the witness stand. McCool unlocked one of his handcuffs, passed it under the railing in front of the witness stand, and relocked it on Jude's wrist. McCool returned to his seat.

Kissick cleared his throat. It was apparent to Jonas that Jude Wiley was going to be the only witness for the defense. Kissick asked pompously, "What is your name?"

Jude looked at him with some surprise. Then he growled, "Jude Wiley."

"Were you acquainted with the deceased?"

"With who?"

"With the murdered girl. Ruth Mc-Cracken."

"Oh, her. Sure. I knew her."

"When did you see her last?"

"The night she was killed. After the dance."

"And what happened?"

Jude Wiley scowled. "Well, she was what you'd call a tease."

John Gebhardt jumped up. "Your honor, I object. The murdered girl is not on trial."

"Sustained," Jonas said. He looked sternly at Jude. "You will confine yourself to answering the questions put to you."

Jude Wiley scowled again. Kissick repeated, "What happened that night after the dance?"

"Well, she'd been flirtin' with me all night."

A titter went around the courtroom, and Jude's face darkened with anger. His glance swept the courtroom. "Well, by God, it's true. She was a goddam floosie!"

Jonas slammed the gavel down. "That will be all of that!"

Jude glowered at him. Jonas looked at Kissick. "Proceed."

Kissick said, "I don't know how I can proceed, your honor, if you won't let my witness testify." He was young and scared, but he was offended too. He said, "The character of the murdered girl is very much an issue here. The defense contends that she flirted with others besides Jude Wiley at that dance. We also contend that she rejected the others as contemptuously as she rejected Jude."

Jonas nodded. Kissick turned to Jude again. "And you left the dance with her. Is that correct?"

Jude nodded. "Sure. That's right."

"And what happened then?"

"Well, we got about a block away an' I put my arms around her."

"Did she respond?"

"Did she what?"

"Did she act as if she liked it?"

Jude shook his head. "No, sir. She acted like a bitch. Reached up and scratched my face. Struggled like a yearlin' heifer."

"Did she say anything?"

"She sure as hell did. Called me a filthy pig. Said I smelled."

"What did you do then?"

"I held onto her. I was mad. I asked her why the hell she'd been flirtin' with me all night if that was the way she felt."

"And what did she say to that?"

"Said I was crazy. Said she hadn't flirted

with me at all."

"And then what?"

"Why I said to hell with you, you slut. I let her go and I got my horse and went on home."

"And what did Ruth do?"

"How the hell do I know what she did? I left her there."

Kissick looked at Gebhardt. "Cross-examine."

Gebhardt walked to the witness stand. "Your father is in jail, isn't he?"

Jude nodded.

"Why is he in jail?"

"The sheriff said he threatened one of them jurors. But it ain't so."

"And you were there when your brothers visited him yesterday, weren't you?"

"You know I was."

"What was discussed?"

Kissick jumped up. "This is not a proper line of questioning."

Jonas looked at Gebhardt. "I agree. What are you trying to establish?"

"That Solomon Wiley gave orders to his sons to kidnap your daughter, Judge."

"That has nothing to do with the issue here."

Gebhardt looked at him reproachfully, as

if thinking that Jonas himself had brought Susan's kidnaping into the trial and was now denying him the right to prove it. He turned back to the witness. "Did Ruth McCracken scratch your face?"

"She sure did."

"How did that make you feel?"

"What do you mean, how did it make me feel? It hurt."

"And it made you mad?"

"Sure it did. She'd been leadin' me on all night. Then when I take her up on it, she digs her claws in me."

"And then you hit her."

Jude glared at him. "The hell I did! I left her just like I said."

"Left her dying. Is that what you mean?"

"No it ain't."

"You were the last one to see her. Until the sheriff found her dying a block away from the place the dance was held."

"Somebody else must've seen her. After I did."

"You can't prove that."

"You can't prove they didn't."

"Nobody else in town had scratches on his face."

"I never denied she scratched me. I said she did."

"And that's when you started beating her."

Jonas interrupted. "You're badgering him, Mr. Gebhardt. And you're getting nowhere."

Gebhardt reddened slightly. He said, "That's all," and walked back to his seat.

Sam McCool came forward and unlocked one of Jude's handcuffs so that he could release him from the rail. He relocked it and led Jude back to his seat.

Jonas looked at Kissick. "Are you ready for your summation?"

"Yes, your honor." Kissick got to his feet and walked to the jury box. He said, "Jude Wiley is on trial for murder. But there were no witnesses and the evidence is circumstantial. Any other man would not even have been brought to trial on the flimsy evidence the prosecution has. But Jude is a member of the Wiley clan. That unwashed family of outcasts that lives at the head of Canyon Creek.

"Oh yes. The people in the town of Canyon Creek hate the Wiley family. But they don't hate them enough to refuse their money when they come to town."

Jonas listened to the amateurish summation with only a part of his mind. With the other he was thinking that the summations of both attorneys would signal the end of the trial. After that, it would be up to him to instruct the jury.

He could recess the court for dinner at the conclusion of Kissick's summation. He could reconvene court at two o'clock, or even at three. But before the day was over, he was going to have to instruct the jury. And if he did not instruct them to bring in a verdict of not guilty, then Susan was going to die.

Kissick droned on. Contrary to his statement that the evidence was circumstantial and flimsy, it was damning and adequate. Ruth McCracken's dying statement had named Jude as her killer and it was generally conceded that people who know they are dying do not lie. The marks of her nails had been on Jude Wiley's face.

But didn't Kissick's summation, however inadequate, give him the excuse he needed to instruct the jury to find Jude not guilty of killing her? He was sorely tempted to grasp that straw. Yet a core of anger remained in him, anger at the way the law, personified by him, had been humiliated on the road to the Wiley ranch.

Frowning, he tried to sort truth from lie, honesty from dishonesty within himself. He kept telling himself that the law had been humiliated. But was his outrage because of the law's humiliation or because of his own? And could he afford to let anger at the way he had been treated color his judgment when Susan's life was at stake?

He knew that he could not. Kissick concluded his lengthy summation lamely and sat down. For an instant there was complete silence in the courtroom as everybody looked toward the judge.

Jonas glanced at John Gebhardt. Gebhardt was taking a last look at his notes. He was prepared to begin right now.

But Jonas knew he had to have more time. His mind was not made up. He said, "It is nearing the dinner hour. Court will recess until two o'clock."

Immediately there was a babble of voices. The bailiff said, "All rise," and the courtroom spectators got noisily to their feet. Jonas went into his chambers.

Enough errors had been made in this trial, he thought, to ensure his verdict being overturned by a higher court if ever the verdict was appealed. But it wouldn't be appealed. Not in the usual sense at least.

If Jude was found guilty, the Wileys would resort to violence. That was a virtual certainty.

Frowning, Jonas began to pace nervously back and forth. He had sometimes wished, while his wife was alive, that he had her faith, her ability to turn to God for help. But he hadn't, and now it was too late. If there was to be any help for him, it would have to come from within himself.

Chapter 15

Jonas Fuller had been in his chambers only a couple of minutes before he heard a knock on the door. Warily he called, "Come in." He was relieved to see Sam McCool. He said, "Come in, Sam."

McCool said, "I had Karl take Jude back to his cell. I wanted to talk to you."

Jonas nodded. "Fire away."

McCool asked, "Why don't you try to get a U.S. marshal here?"

"How?" Jonas asked.

"Jury tampering is a federal crime. Why don't you telegraph Denver and see?"

Jonas nodded. "I never thought of that, but I guess you're right. I'll go down and send the telegram right away. Not that he could get here in time to do us any good. Jude's trial is over with, except for

Gebhardt's summation. I'm going to have to instruct the jury this afternoon.''

''It won't hurt to have a marshal on the way.''

Jonas nodded.

McCool looked relieved. He went out, closing the door behind him.

Jonas put on his hat. He felt twenty years older than he really was. He was desperately worried about Susan, and his virtually sleepless night had begun to tell on him.

He walked along the courthouse corridor and down the stairs. There was still a crowd out front. People stood in little groups, discussing the case, speculating on what the jury's verdict was going to be. Jonas heard one man say, ''They'll never find him guilty, because they're all afraid. When the Wileys threatened Clay and Pew, they threatened all the jurors and the jury knows it.''

Jonas went on. What the man had said was true. And so perhaps his concern about what he was going to do was unnecessary, even absurd. The jury's verdict had probably been decided by the Wiley family. It wasn't going to matter how he instructed them.

He frowned at his own thoughts, knowing that kind of thinking was just an easy way out of the dilemma facing him. He hurried along the street in the direction of the railroad depot, unaware that a block behind him Andrew and Simon Wiley were following.

He reached the depot. It was deserted, except that a little plume of smoke came from the tin chimney above the cubicle where the telegraph office was. He stepped up on the platform and crossed it, his steps sounding hollowly.

Art Tobias, wearing a green eyeshade, his sleeves held by elastic bands, glanced up as Jonas came in the door. He said, with startled surprise, "Judge Fuller! What brings you down here?"

Jonas nodded. "Hello, Art. I want to send a telegram."

Tobias got up, his back bent, wearing a shiny vest and an equally shiny black bow tie. He shoved a pad of telegram blanks and a pencil toward Jonas.

Jonas addressed his telegram to the United States Marshal's Office in Denver. He wrote, URGENTLY NEED HELP OF U. S. MARSHAL IMMEDIATELY. JURY TRYING A MURDER CASE HAS BEEN THREATENED AND INTIMIDATED AS HAS THE JUDGE. REPLY AT ONCE. He signed his name, JONAS FULLER, JUDGE.

He had just finished, and had shoved the

pad toward Tobias when he heard the door. Turning his head, he saw Andrew and Simon Wiley come through the door. Andrew crossed the room. Simon closed the door and stood with his back to it.

Andrew reached for the pad that Jonas had shoved toward the telegrapher. Jonas caught his arm. "Get your hands away from that."

Andrew shook off his hand. He seized the pad and pulled it toward him. Squinting slightly and reading with difficulty, he said, "This says, 'U. S. Marshal's Office, Denver.'" He turned his head and looked at Simon.

"What else does it say?"

Frowning, Andrew stared down at the pad. "It says, 'Ur . . . gently . . . need . . . help . . . of . . . U. S. Marshal . . . imm . . . ediately. Jury . . . trying . . . murder case has been . . . threatened and . . . intim . . .'" He looked helplessly at his brother. Simon said, "Intimidated."

Andrew went on: "'as . . . has . . . the judge.'" He looked at Jonas. "You been intimidated, Judge?"

Jonas reached out and seized the pad. Andrew held onto it, pulling it away from him. He tore off the top sheet and deliberately shredded it, afterward letting the scraps fall to the floor at his feet.

Jonas felt his anger rise. He looked at Tobias. "You know what the message said. Send it."

Tobias nodded. He left the counter and went to his instrument. It began to click busily.

Andrew came swiftly around the counter. He knocked Tobias's chair over with a sweep of his arm. He caught the table which held the telegrapher's instruments by its edge and overturned it with a crash. From the door Simon said, "Rip out the wires too."

Tobias struggled to his feet, his face gray with fear. He backed into a corner and stood there cowering. He looked at Jonas, as if expecting protection from the law. Jonas said, "I intend to have you both arrested as soon as court convenes this afternoon."

Andrew, busy ripping out wires, turned his head and stared arrogantly at him. "You don't care too much about that girl of yours, do you, Judge?"

Jonas felt the blood draining from his face. He went around the end of the counter and crossed to where Tobias stood. "Are you hurt?"

Tobias shook his head, his eyes clinging

fearfully to the Wiley brothers. Jonas asked, "Can you repair your instrument?"

Tobias nodded mutely.

"How long will it take?"

"An hour. Maybe more."

"Get at it. I want you to send that telegram."

Tobias shook his head, his eyes still clinging to the grinning faces of Simon and Andrew. Andrew chuckled. "You see, Judge? Everybody ain't stupid, the way you are."

"I can send a messenger down the line to the next telegraph station."

Andrew nodded. "You do that. We'll catch him before he goes a mile."

Jonas asked in desperation, "Does your father know you're doing this?"

"How could he? He's in jail. But he ain't going to be there long. Soon's you turn Jude loose . . . well, you ain't goin' to get that girl of yours back 'til you turn Pa loose too."

Jonas headed for the door. "I'm going after the sheriff."

Like one boy tormenting another, Andrew stuck out a foot. It tripped Jonas and he sprawled headlong onto the oiled wood floor. He was stunned for a moment, but he was both angered and humiliated too. He

170

struggled to his feet. Andrew and Simon were grinning mockingly at him.

Never in his life had Jonas wanted more to resort to physical violence. Never before had he so wanted to take the law into his own hands. Right now he was capable of killing, he thought with a shock. Had a weapon been available to him, he would have used it unhesitatingly. He glanced toward Tobias. ''Get your instrument fixed as soon as you can.''

Tobias shook his head. ''Huh-uh, Judge. Not me. I'm closin' up for the day an' goin' home.''

He scurried to the coat tree and took down his coat and hat. He literally ran out of the office, giving the two Wiley brothers as wide a berth as possible. He ran across the station platform, jumped down into the dusty street and ran until he disappeared.

Andrew Wiley said, ''Now there's a man that's got some sense.''

Jonas knew it was useless to argue, useless to threaten, useless to say anything. He asked, ''Are you through with me?''

Andrew looked at Simon, grinning. ''Are we through with him?''

Simon stared at the judge, grinning the same way his brother was. He remained silent for a long, long time, as though trying to think of some other indignity he could inflict. Reluctantly then he nodded his head. "I guess we are."

Jonas went out. He was furious but he knew there wasn't a thing that he could do. He could have Sam McCool try arresting Andrew and Simon when court convened this afternoon, but he knew he wouldn't. The law had been humiliated enough here in Canyon Creek. If the Wileys resisted Sam when he tried arresting them and if they killed him, it would be the end of the rule of law. After that the Wileys would do as they pleased and nobody would dare protest.

Furthermore, if he had Andrew and Simon arrested, it would only increase Susan's danger. And she was in danger enough without him adding any more to it.

Besides, he told himself, his humiliation at the railroad depot and the destruction of the telegrapher's equipment was a small matter compared to what really was at stake. If the main battle against the Wileys could be won, Andrew and Simon could be arrested any time.

But how was the main battle going to be won? The heart had gone out of the jurymen. He himself was afraid to take a stand because he knew if he did he'd never see Susan again.

It was ridiculous, he thought, that a small handful of lawless men could so intimidate an entire community. There were enough able-bodied men in the county to form a posse sufficiently large to enforce the law against the Wiley family. The trouble was, the Wileys had convinced them of the danger of co-operating with the law. They had burned Bill Clay's house. They had threatened Pew. And they had kidnaped the daughter of the judge, thereby convincing the people that no one was safe from them.

Jonas passed the restaurant. The smell of the food made him feel slightly ill. He knew he ought to eat, but he also knew that he could not. He had gone no more than a dozen steps when he heard Sam McCool call out to him. He turned.

Sam had several trays stacked up in his hands. Jonas took two of them, then walked toward the courthouse with Sam. Sam asked, "Get the telegram sent?"

Jonas shook his head.

"Why not?"

"Andrew and Simon Wiley."

"By God, they're going to go too far. Where are they now?"

Jonas said, "Let them alone. They roughed Art Tobias and me up and they destroyed some telegraph equipment but they can pay for that any time. Right now we've got more important things to worry about."

"If I let them get away with something like that, no telling what they'll do next."

"I didn't say to let them get away with it. I just said to wait."

"Somebody's got to show them . . ."

"They're pretty arrogant and Solomon can't keep them in check because he's in jail. What if they were to resist? What if you got killed?"

"Do you think I'm afraid of that?"

Jonas shook his head.

McCool studied the judge's face. "All right. You know what you want. Have you decided what you're going to do? About Jude, I mean."

Jonas didn't reply immediately. The arrogance of the two Wileys at the railroad depot had come closer to convincing him of what he ought to do than anything had done so far.

It was true that Susan's life was in jeopardy. But if he surrendered to the Wileys' intimidation, no girl, no woman would henceforth be safe from them. Nor

174

would any man or any property.

On the other hand, if he did his duty and instructed the jury properly, and if Jude was found guilty and sentenced to be hanged, then a confrontation with the entire Wiley clan was inevitable. A lot of people might get killed.

He said suddenly, "I'm going to have to fight them, Sam. It's what Susan wanted me to do when she told me about the threat."

They reached the courthouse. Jonas carried the trays down the stairs and into the sheriff's office. Sam McCool followed him. He said, "You're doing right, Jonas. You're doing the only thing you can. If you did anything else, we'd just as well let them have the whole shebang."

Jonas nodded unenthusiastically and climbed the stairs. He reached his chambers, went in and closed the door. He sat down, put his feet up on the desk, laid his head back and closed his eyes.

He was praying silently, that he had decided right, that Susan would not suffer because of what he would do this afternoon.

But he felt as if he had just signed her death warrant and he felt sure he would never see her again alive.

Chapter 16

At two, Jake Tipton knocked lightly on the judge's door. He opened it slightly, stuck his head in and said, "Two o'clock, Judge."

Jonas got out of his chair. Almost as though in a daze, he went into the courtroom and sat down behind the bench. He said, "Court is in session." He glanced at John Gebhardt. "Are you ready for your summation?"

"Yes, your honor." Gebhardt got up. His summation was brief and to the point. He cited the evidence he had presented, the dying testimony of the murdered girl, the scratches on Jude Wiley's face, the flesh found under the girl's fingernails. He cited witnesses' testimony that Jude had followed Ruth McCracken away from the dance and Jude's own admission that this was so. He demanded that the jury find Jude guilty of murder in the first degree, and he demanded the death penalty.

Finished, he sat down. Jonas looked at the jurymen. Now was the moment he had dreaded so. The Wileys were looking at him expectantly, triumphant smiles upon their faces.

He began his instructions to the jury, and he found himself using all the routine words. He instructed them to consider only the evidence that had been presented. He did not instruct them to bring in a verdict of not guilty, and he could see the Wileys' triumphant smiles turning to scowls of anger. Finally he said, "This court has been subject to disruption and intimidation. Jurors have been threatened." He paused while he looked at each juror successively. "These tactics must not be permitted to influence the proceedings of the court. You must not bring in a verdict of guilty simply because you are angry over the threats. Nor can you find Jude Wiley innocent because you are afraid. This community stands at a crossroads. Only if you arrive at an impartial verdict based wholly on the evidence, can the community survive and only then can the law survive." He nodded to the bailiff. "Conduct the jury to the jury room."

The jury filed out of the courtroom. The Wiley men remained seated as if overpoweringly confident the jury would be back with their verdict immediately. The other members of the family, women, children, boys, got to their feet and filed out of the courtroom. They were going home, Jonas realized. Having put on a show of solidarity and support for Jude, they now had no further reason to stay.

He beckoned to Jake Tipton. "Tell the sheriff I want to see him in my chambers immediately."

"Yes, your honor." Jake headed for McCool who, with Karl Burbach, was escorting Jude Wiley from the room.

Jonas retired into his chambers and closed the door. He was more deeply troubled than ever before in his life. Always before, right and wrong had been clear-cut and plain. Now, suddenly, they were confused. By doing his duty, he had, perhaps, sacrificed Susan's life.

But he had done his duty, and now he could put the trial out of his mind. What happened was in the jury's hands. If they were afraid—if the Wileys' threats had indeed intimidated them, then they would return a not guilty verdict and Jude Wiley would go free. But if they did their duty fearlessly, Jude would be found guilty and Jonas would ultimately sentence him to death.

He heard a knock on the door and called, "Come in, Sam."

Sam McCool came in. There was an abundance of approval in his eyes and it warmed Jonas to see it there. McCool said, "Judge, you did this county proud. Now if the jury will do as well . . ."

Jonas asked, "Do you think they will? Do you think they'll find him guilty, Sam?"

The sheriff shrugged. "Hell, I don't know. But I'll bet you one thing. They won't be coming in with a verdict right away. They'll be out all night and maybe all day tomorrow."

Jonas nodded. "That's the way I figured it. I also figured the Wileys would stay in town until the jury did come in."

McCool grinned. "They're sitting out there in the courtroom waiting as if they expected the jury to come back right away."

Jonas said, "I did what I had to out there, Sam. I did my duty for the community. Now I've got to do something for myself."

Sam stared questioningly at him. "What do you mean?"

"I mean I'm going to get Susan away from them."

Sam stared unbelievingly at him. "Are you out of your mind?"

"She's out there, Sam. The guard up in the rocks admitted it."

"But how . . . ? You know how impossible it is to get in there. You tried going in by the road and it didn't work. There's only one other trail and that's guarded too."

"Does a man have to have a trail? When I was a kid back in Iowa we had a tree house. We climbed up the tree to get to it, but climbing down was too slow so we had a rope. We slid down it to the ground."

"You're not seriously suggesting that we slide off that rim on a rope?"

"That's exactly what I'm suggesting, Sam. Only I hadn't gotten to the 'we' part of it yet."

"You don't think for a minute that I'd let you go in there alone?"

"It's pretty risky, Sam. There's not much more than one chance in ten we'll ever get out of there alive."

McCool didn't acknowledge that. He

asked, "How far down do you suppose it is?"

"We'd better have five hundred feet of rope."

"That's what I was thinking. I'll go down to the lumber yard and see if they've got that much on hand."

"I'll go home and change. I'll saddle up and meet you there in half an hour. If we can get out of town by four o'clock, we ought to be on top of that rim at dusk. We can get off the rim and down to the canyon floor before it gets completely dark."

McCool stared at him a moment, as if unable to believe what he said. Then he turned and left, going out into the corridor instead of into the courtroom where the Wileys were.

Jonas opened the door slightly and looked into the courtroom. He could see the sons of Solomon Wiley sitting there. Two of them were smoking, Andrew and Simon. Thomas leaned forward, elbows on knees, scowling at the floor.

Nothing was going to happen while he was gone, Jonas thought. The Wileys wouldn't try breaking Jude and their father out of jail while there was still a chance Jude would be found innocent. And even if the jury reached a verdict sooner than he expected, they'd have to keep it to themselves until he returned.

He closed the door, put on his hat and left by the corridor door as the sheriff had. He went downstairs, relieved to see that most of the crowd had scattered and gone home. The last of the Wiley wives and children in their ramshackle vehicle was just turning the corner, heading for the Canyon Creek road.

Jonas hurried home, his thoughts on Susan now. She'd be safe enough, he thought, until the verdict was in. The Wileys would wait until they saw what the jury did before harming her. That gave him all night to rescue her.

He walked briskly, feeling more alert, more alive than he had in a long, long time. He didn't let himself consider the odds against rescuing Susan successfully. Nor did he think how perilous it was to try sliding down five hundred feet of rope in uncertain light. If he had, he would have realized that his muscles, at fifty-seven, might well give out long before he reached the bottom of the rope. He wasn't in the best of shape. A judge's life is sedentary and he doesn't get much exercise.

He reached home. Quickly he stuffed

some food into his mouth, washing it down with cold coffee, strong and bitter from being two days in the pot. Still eating, he changed his clothes, putting on old ones that he used when he worked out in the yard. He found some old boots that he'd used on occasional hunting trips, and a broad-brimmed hat.

He finished eating, and went out to the stable. He saddled up the buggy horse, mounted and rode down the alley toward the center of town. He took a roundabout route, hoping he would not be recognized. He reached the alley behind the lumber yard, to find Sam waiting, a huge coil of rope tied behind his saddle.

Sam swung to the saddle immediately. He had a rifle in his saddle boot and his customary revolver belted around his waist. He handed Jonas a revolver, which Jonas stuffed down into his belt.

McCool rode down the alley at a trot. Reaching the bed of Canyon Creek, he followed it for a couple of miles until the two were well clear of town and the scattered dwellings that surrounded it. Then he climbed his horse out onto level ground and headed north.

Now that he was committed to doing this,

Jonas found he was almost unable to take his eyes off the coil of rope. He'd never be able to slide down five hundred feet of rope to the bottom of the rim. He'd scrape the rock wall all the way and before he was halfway down his muscles would give out and he would fall the rest of the way to his death.

And even if the two of them did get safely down, what could they really do? How could they find the building where Susan was being held prisoner? And if by some miracle they did, how could they rescue her from it and get her out of the Wiley stronghold alive? They sure as hell couldn't go up the rope. And they couldn't get out by the road. Not with that guard up there in the rocks.

Idly Jonas wondered how the Wileys guarded that road at night. They probably strung a cable across the road. And they probably moved their guards down into the rocks close to the road.

The sun slid toward the horizon in the west. The land here was rough, consisting of a rising series of rounded, sagebrush-covered hills. Each had to be climbed and descended on the other side. Occasionally they had to follow a ravine for half a mile or more, hunting a crossing. McCool, plainly worried about the time, began to spur his horse impatiently.

They were passing through cedars now, and piñon pine, and at last Jonas saw a low line of rimrock ahead of him. McCool galloped his horse across a level area half a mile wide, then spurred him up through the crumbled rocks of the shallow rim.

Reaching the top, he halted his horse momentarily. Both animals were soaked with sweat; both were heaving from the climb. Impatiently, McCool waited for the horses' breathing to become normal again. Jonas asked, "How far is it now?"

"Couple of miles. But we're just about out of time." He glanced westward at the orange ball of sun sliding even now below the horizon.

McCool waited a few moments more. Then he touched his horse's sides with his spurs and the horse broke into a steady lope across what now was fairly level land. Jonas followed a dozen yards behind, staring at the coil of rope with something close to fascination. He was scared. He admitted it. But he knew when the rope was dropped over the rim, he'd go down. No matter what happened or how scared he was, he'd go down.

McCool finally yanked his horse to a plunging halt. They were in timber now, among huge, thick-trunked yellow pines. Here and there the leaves of a yellow quakie trembled in the breeze. McCool said, "Tie up your reins. The horses will go back to town."

Jonas tied up his reins. McCool untied the coil of rope and slapped his horse on the rump. Then, followed by Jonas, he walked to the lip of the rim.

Jonas stared down into the void, a sinking feeling growing in the pit of his stomach. It looked like a mile straight down.

The valley was in shadow now, and everything down there was tinged with purplish gray. Jonas could see the cluster of buildings so far away they looked like toys. He saw no movement in the yard, but he heard the distant bark of a dog, answered by another one.

McCool tied the end of the rope around a tree. Then, so that it would not be tangled halfway down, he fed the other end over the precipice. He said, "I'll go down first."

Jonas shook his head. "Huh-uh. It's my idea. I'm going first."

"The rope may not be long enough. I

never measured this damn rim. I only guessed.''

Jonas grinned. ''If it isn't long enough, I'll climb back up.''

McCool took two pairs of new leather gloves from his pocket. He handed one pair to Jonas, who immediately put them on.

Jonas's knees felt weak. They were trembling and he hoped McCool couldn't see. He walked to the edge of the precipice, and grasped the rope. He eased himself over, refusing to look down, knowing that if he did his courage might disappear.

The rope laid against the rock wall and it was hard getting his legs wrapped around it. He managed and began the descent. He heard McCool softly call, ''Good luck.''

Jonas said between his teeth, ''If the rope's too short, I'll yell before I drop. If you don't hear me yell after that, don't try coming down.''

McCool gave him no reply. Jonas let himself begin the slide, trying to keep from going down too fast. He could already feel the strength in his arms diminishing. And a cold terror settled in his heart.

Chapter 17

The chasm yawned beneath him. Despite his determination not to look down, Jonas found the compulsion to do so irresistible. He glanced down and felt suddenly as though there was a vacuum in his chest. It looked as if five hundred miles yawned below him instead of five hundred feet. And suddenly he was sure that the rope was much too short. He would reach its end and, unable to go back up, would be left with no alternative but to drop to his death. Sam McCool couldn't haul him up. Not without a horse. Besides that, the end of the rope was tied to a tree. Even if he had a horse, Sam would be unable to untie it and then secure it to the saddle horn.

Jonas realized that he had stopped sliding, that he now was gripping the rope with all his strength. He forced himself to relax his grip, and to let the rope slip through his hands. He began once more slowly to descend.

After a while, he looked up. He was startled to observe that he had descended less than fifty feet. And already his strength was beginning to wane.

He relaxed his hands even more and plunged swiftly down. The rope, slipping through his gloved hands, heated the gloves so much that he could smell them scorching. He tightened his hands, tightened the grip of his legs and feet on the rope, and began to slow.

Once more he looked down, horrified at how far he still had to go. He could see the rope dangling below him, whipping back and forth from the motion imparted to it by his descent, but he could not see its end. It was getting too dark for that.

A new and equally horrifying thought occurred to him. Suppose he reached the end of the rope without seeing it? Besides plunging to his own death, he would be unable to warn McCool. The sheriff would come down the rope and suffer a similar fate because he had not been warned.

Slowly he went on, glancing neither up nor

down, steeling himself against the panic that threatened to engulf his mind. Panic would help no one. It could certainly get him killed.

He tried to think of Susan and he discovered that doing so calmed him. But he was tiring. He knew it and he didn't know how much longer he could continue to grip the rope. Furthermore, he no longer dared to speed his descent. Only by going down slowly could he make sure he knew it when he came to the end of the rope.

Occasionally he loosened a rock from the face of the cliff and it fell, to strike the slide far below. From there it bounded downward until it reached the cedars at the foot of the slide. He wondered briefly if the sounds would alert the Wiley family. He doubted it. Rocks fell off the rim all the time, loosened by rain, freezing or wind. They probably would pay no attention to the sounds.

His hands and arms now felt almost completely numb. And despite his efforts not to, he felt himself beginning to pick up speed. The rope literally hissed through his hands. He tried to grip harder with legs and feet and discovered they were almost as numb as were his arms.

This was it, he thought. He had tried but he had failed. He now was plummeting down at a rate that guaranteed he would miss the end of the rope when it came. His only hope was that the rope was long enough, that he would reach solid ground before he ran out of rope.

He felt himself plummet into space and uttered a high yell of panic and alarm. For an instant he felt suspended there, and then he struck the slide with an impact that knocked some of the wind out of him. Helplessly gasping, he rolled over and over down the slide, loosening rocks until a veritable avalanche accompanied his descent, raising a cloud of dust that would surely have been seen by some of the Wileys if it had not already been so dark.

He slammed against an enormous rock imbedded in the slide, and lay there stunned for several moments while the avalanche of loose rocks came tumbling down past him and over him. He felt in his belt, reassured that the gun was still in place.

He thought of Sam. Looking up toward the top of the rim, towering high above, he shouted, "Sam? Come on!" and hoped his voice had been loud enough for Sam to hear while not being loud enough for the Wiley family's ears.

He couldn't see the rope at all, but he saw

Sam's shadowy form against the top of the rim, saw it begin to descend. He wanted to warn Sam of the fall from the end of the rope, but he doubted if Sam could make out his words. And he didn't want to risk being heard by members of the Wiley family.

Straining his eyes to see through the increasing gloom, he followed Sam's progress downward. Sam's arms and hands must be stronger than his had been, he thought, because Sam was descending at a regular and deliberate rate of speed. When he judged Sam was near the end of the rope, Jonas softly called, "You'll drop fifteen or twenty feet."

There was utter silence for a moment after that. Then he heard Sam gasp, and an instant later heard the crash as Sam struck the slide at the base of the rim. Sam came rolling toward him, as helpless as he himself had been.

Seeing that Sam would miss the rock that had stopped his own descent, he moved his body out away from it and into Sam's path, still holding to the rock. The sheriff's blocky body struck him, nearly ripping loose his grip on the imbedded rock. Then Sam McCool was clawing at the slide, spread-eagled on his belly. He stopped, held in place precariously by Jonas's legs and by his own fingers digging into the loose rock and earth.

Slowly, slowly, he worked himself over behind the rock. He said fervently, "Whew! I hope I never have to do anything like that again."

Jonas could only think that he had given himself up for dead and that now he was alive. He said, "We made it! By God, we made it! I didn't think we would."

"You hurt?"

Jonas stood up, bracing himself against the rock. There was a twinge of pain in his right leg, but he could put his weight on it. He tried both arms, relieved that they both worked properly.

He knew his clothes were torn. His hat was gone. He had sustained so many cuts and bruises that his whole body burned. But he was alive and functioning. He said, "No. I'm not hurt. Are you?"

McCool stood up beside him, also testing arms and legs. He said, "No, but I lost that damn rifle in the fall. I had it tied to my back."

It still was not quite dark. Enough gray light remained in the sky to see the jagged silhouette of the rim five hundred feet above, but there was not enough light to see objects on the ground. Jonas said, "You'll never find it in the dark. Have you still got the other gun?"

McCool groped for and found the butt of his holstered gun. He said, "Uh-huh. Let's go."

Carefully, digging each foot successively into the loose earth and rock, he began to descend. Cautiously, his knees still trembling, Jonas followed him. They were a pair of fools, he thought. Two middle-aged men invading the stronghold of an outfit like the Wiley family. Then he grinned faintly to himself. The worst was over. They had made it down the rim. After that hair-raising descent, anything else ought to be child's play.

They were, he judged, half to three quarters of a mile from the buildings of the Wiley ranch. A cautious step at a time they descended the slide. When they reached its foot, the sky was wholly dark. There must be a thin overcast, Jonas thought, because only a few stars were dimly visible.

Ahead stretched a half mile of rounded, cedar-covered hills. Beyond them was the valley floor and somewhere in the middle of that was Canyon Creek. Jonas thought about what it would be like to bury his face in that cold, clear stream.

Sam McCool moved away through the cedars, saying softly as he did, "We've got a couple of hours, at least. We don't want to do much of anything until they're all asleep."

Jonas did not reply. The difficulties facing them seemed insurmountable. They had to reach the Wiley buildings without being seen. Somehow they had to discover in which one of them Susan was being held prisoner. After that they had to overpower the guard and rescue her.

But that part would be easy compared with what came afterward. Having overpowered the guard and rescued her, they then would have to get her out of the canyon past the guards stationed along the road.

Jonas wondered whether the jury had reached a decision yet. He doubted it. He wondered how long it would take their horses to get back to town. It could take all night. It could take a week or more. But even if the horses reached town by morning, no help would be forthcoming from the people of the town. They were afraid of the Wiley family. With no leadership they'd simply close their eyes to the possibility that both the sheriff and the judge had been killed.

But if the horses should reach town, and if the town's inhabitants wanted to do something, guessing where the judge and sheriff had gone should be relatively simple for them. Anthony Lambert, at the lumber yard, would tell them about the five hundred feet of rope. No one would have trouble guessing what that was for. They would know the sheriff and the judge had descended into the Wiley stronghold from the top of the rim. And that would explain to them the riderless horses that had reached town with their reins tied up.

Jonas stumbled on a down log and fell. Cursing softly, he struggled to his feet. He was surprised to realize that despite the long ride from town, despite the descent on the rope and the fall from its end, he was not as weary as he had expected to be. Excitement was a stimulant, he thought. Even for a man who is fifty-seven years old and who has lived a largely sedentary life.

Eventually, after more than half an hour of cautious traveling through the cedars, they reached a knoll from which they could look out across the valley floor.

Some cattle got up ahead of them and

trotted through the sagebrush toward the creek. After listening a while for other sounds, Sam led the way down the last steep hill.

Moving like shadows, they crossed the two-track road that the Wileys used getting haying machinery to their upper fields. They moved through the head-high sagebrush. Once again they startled a small bunch of cattle and the cattle trotted away in front of them.

At the stream, Jonas fell to his knees. He laid out prone and put his face into the water. He sucked up the icy water thirstily. McCool also drank. Then he led out again, angling back across the sagebrush flat for the high ground above the untidily scattered collection of buildings.

Stars were no longer visible, and Jonas knew that clouds had moved thickly across the sky. The air, he suddenly noticed, was much cooler than it had been on other recent nights. A chill wind blew out of the north.

They could see lights twinkling from the windows now, even though they still were nearly half a mile away. Jonas asked worriedly, "What about dogs? They're sure to have a lot of dogs."

McCool said wryly, "Dogs are all I've

been thinkin' about for the last half hour. If we get done in, it will be by dogs.''

"Maybe they won't pay any attention to us. There are so damn many people living in that bunch of shacks down there. Must be fifty or sixty. Is a dog going to notice a stranger among all those?''

McCool chuckled. ''Up close, yes. But maybe they won't pay any attention to us just walking around down there.''

They reached a vantage point about two hundred yards from the nearest house. Absently Jonas counted all the buildings he could see. There were twenty-five. And suddenly the task they had set themselves seemed totally impossible. How were they going to determine where Susan was being held?

Sam said, ''I think we ought to split up. You stay here and I'll work my way around to the other side. We'll have a better chance that way of finding out where she is.''

Jonas agreed. Sam got up and cautiously moved away through the sagebrush. He disappeared almost instantly, like a shadow.

Jonas wished he knew what time it was. He pulled out his watch and tried to see its face but it was too dark. And he didn't dare light a match.

A light in one of the houses went out. He heard a door slam. A tomcat began caterwauling and a voice shouted angrily at him to shut up. Something was thrown that sounded like a metal pan. It rattled along the ground, but the cat did not stop.

Another door slammed open, throwing a square of light upon the ground in front of it. A woman screeched curses at the cat, without results. A dog began to bark.

Jonas narrowed his eyes. Another door opened and a woman came out and disappeared into the darkness immediately. Where had she gone, and why, Jonas wondered. After several moments she returned. "The outhouse," he thought.

He wondered if Sam had reached the other side of the place. And he waited, growing a little colder every time a light went out. If they didn't find out where Susan was before all the lights went out, they weren't going to find out where she was. It was as simple as that.

Chapter 18

More lights winked out in the buildings just below. Jonas continued to fidget nervously. Finally, knowing this was a risk he had to take, he moved closer so that he could see. But he discovered that the closer he moved, the less he was able to see because buildings got in the way.

Frustrated, he backed away again and began pacing back and forth about three hundred yards from the nearest building. More lights went out. Another door opened and a woman came out of it. Jonas glanced briefly at her, then looked away.

Suddenly his glance went back to her. She was heading straight across the yard. She was not heading toward the nearest outhouse at all.

She disappeared from his view, then

reappeared again in the faint light thrown from a window, then disappeared again. Anxiously, Jonas moved closer, following her as she walked but staying almost three hundred yards away. She had disappeared into the darkness again, then had gone behind a building, but now she reappeared, a dim, shadowy blur against the weather-whitened side of an enormous barn. Where the hell was she going, he asked himself. Then he heard her voice, to be answered by the deeper voice of a boy who sounded as if he might be thirteen or fourteen years old.

Jonas moved closer cautiously. He could now see two people standing in front of a low log building backed up to a hillside on the near side of the yard. He heard the door creak open, and heard the woman's voice again, to be answered by another woman's voice that he recognized instantly as Susan's, even though he could not understand her words.

He froze where he stood, not now wanting to risk discovery either by the woman or the boy, or by any dogs that might be prowling around in the dark. He saw the woman and a slighter figure, that must be Susan, cross the yard in the direction from which the woman just had come. They disappeared.

The shadowy figure of the boy remained by the open door.

Elation surged wildly in Jonas Fuller's mind. Susan was all right, and he had found the place they were keeping her. The woman had obviously come to escort her to the outhouse before retiring, judging perhaps that it was not a proper task for a half-grown boy.

He backed away from the small log building, returning to the spot where he'd been when Sam McCool left to go around to the other side. He vaguely saw the two figures returning. Once more he heard the voices of the woman and the boy. Then he heard the door creak shut.

Desperately he wished he could let Susan know that he was here. She must be terrified, he thought. But that would have to wait.

Lights kept going out among the buildings until only two were left. Finally these two went out as well and utter darkness settled over the place. Jonas listened intently because he knew Sam would be returning soon. After about twenty minutes, he heard the scuff of a boot and saw a shadowy figure approaching him. He called softly, "Sam? Over here."

The figure turned and came straight

toward him. Sam asked anxiously, "Find out anything?" He was obviously worried because he had not.

Jonas said, "Uh-huh. She's in that log building there. The way it's dug back into the hillside, I'd say it was probably an icehouse. There's a boy watching her. From his voice he sounds about fourteen."

Sam squatted down. "I sure could use a smoke." But he made no move.

Jonas squatted beside him. The cat began to squawl again and a woman's voice scolded the cat shrilly. A dog barked briefly and then was quiet again. Sam muttered, "Damn cat. I hope he doesn't keep doing that all night."

Once more quiet settled over the place. They waited almost half an hour. Then Sam touched Jonas's arm and whispered, "Come on."

Both men got to their feet. Sam whispered, "He won't be expecting anything. These people think no outsider can get in here. I think one of us can walk right up to him, while the other slips up on him from behind, just in case."

Sam added, "I'll approach him from the front. You don't look like any of the Wileys, even in the dark. You're too skinny."

Jonas grinned. Every nerve in his body

was strung tight. His knees had begun to shake again and he cursed them soundlessly for betraying him. Sam said, "I'll go straight in from the direction of the other buildings. I'll have to risk the dogs. You come down from behind the icehouse."

He left Jonas and circled behind the towering ramshackle barn. He disappeared.

Hurrying, but taking care to make no noise, Jonas circled the icehouse, and approached it from the rear. He had almost reached it when he saw Sam's shadowy figure against the weather-whitened wall of the barn. Sam was no more than a dozen yards from the boy standing by the icehouse door.

The icehouse now hid both Sam and the boy from Jonas's view. He circled it and reached the front corner just as the boy said surprisedly, "Hey! Who are you anyway?"

Sam came in low, rushing, and his body hit the boy below the waist. The boy's legs went out from under him and he hit the ground with a thump that drove the air out of him in an explosive gust. He opened his mouth to shout, but no words came out, only the sounds of his frantic attempts to fill his lungs with air. Sam grappled briefly with him, and clamped a big hand over his mouth.

The boy bit his hand and Sam withdrew it with a muttered curse. He drew back his fist and struck the boy, hard, on the side of the jaw. The boy slumped to the ground, limp and unresisting now.

Jonas opened the icehouse door. He said, "Susan? Don't make any noise. It's Sam and me."

There was a flurry of movement in the icehouse and Susan came rushing into his arms. He held her close to him, feeling the violence of her trembling, knowing in this instant how great and how terrible her fear had been. Sam dragged the boy into the icehouse, then came out again and closed the door. He dropped the forked stick into the padlock hasp.

Sam whispered, "Let's get out of here."

Jonas whispered back, "Where are we going? Are we going to get horses?"

"Huh-uh. We'll have a better chance of slipping past that guard on foot. Come on."

He led the way. Jonas pushed Susan into second place and himself brought up the rear. They headed away from the buildings toward town, toward the narrow canyon passage that led to the town of Canyon Creek. Susan, ahead of him, whispered to

Jonas, "How in the world did you get here?"

"Came down the rim."

"Came down the rim?" she repeated unbelievingly. "It's five hundred feet high!"

"We came down on a rope."

"You're not serious!"

"We're serious all right. Be quiet now until we get clear."

Almost silently the three made their way down the valley of Canyon Creek. But they had gone less than five hundred feet from the buildings when a rustling in the brush beside the road made Jonas jump. Almost instantly, two dogs rushed at him, barking furiously. One was big, the other about half his size. The larger one's bark had a hollow sound. The smaller dog's bark was shrill and penetrating. Sam shouted, "Go on ahead! Run! I'll get rid of these goddam dogs!"

Jonas didn't argue with him. He pushed Susan on ahead, running, and following her. But the dogs did not stay to bark at Sam. They followed Susan, still barking furiously.

Jonas lunged at them. He caught the smaller one by a hind leg and the dog began to yelp furiously. Swinging it in an arc, Jonas dashed its head against the ground. It stopped yelping suddenly and he dropped the unconscious animal to the ground.

The other dog was rushing, then darting away, then rushing in again. His barking had taken on a more urgent tone now that Jonas had disposed of the smaller one.

Behind them, in the darkened buildings, lights were coming on. The voices of women shrilled and the voices of half-grown boys yelled excitedly.

Suddenly Sam McCool's gun roared. The big dog, wounded, limped away into the darkness, yelping with pain. Jonas said, "For Christ's sake . . ."

"I know. But I figured the shot might bring the guard out of the canyon. When we see him go by, maybe we can slip past him and get through the canyon before he knows we're gone."

All three were running now. The wounded dog had lost interest, but his yelping provided a point of reference for the pursuit. Ahead, Jonas suddenly heard the pound of a horse's hoofs upon the road and left it immediately, dragging Susan along with him.

Crouching in the brush beside the road, the three saw a man thunder past. He pulled in his horse almost immediately as he came to the place where the wounded dog still yelped, surrounded by a crowd of excited, armed women and boys. A shout lifted, "Hey! Dan ain't here at the icehouse! He's gone!"

A man's voice roared, "Look inside!"

There was a moment's pause. Then the same shout came again, "Dan's inside the goddam thing. He's either unconscious or he's dead!"

The man's voice bawled, "Get lanterns and spread out! I'll close off the canyon entrance. Somebody's here! By God, you find 'em or you know what Pa will do!"

The galloping horse passed again, this time heading toward the canyon mouth. Sam cursed softly and bitterly beneath his breath. He said, "Now we're bottled up."

Jonas whispered, "There's nothing left to do now but hide. And I can't think of a better place for that than the icehouse over there. It will be the last place they look."

Sam agreed. The three ran up on the hillside as silently as they could, circling toward the rear of the log icehouse. They came down behind it cautiously. Sam went ahead. Susan came second. Jonas brought up the rear.

Sam circled the unconscious youth, who had been dragged outside by whoever it was that had discovered him. He was still unconscious. Susan, coming along behind Sam, did not see the boy and stumbled over him. She fell to her knees, uttering an involuntary cry. Jonas grabbed her, lifted her, and shoved her through the icehouse door.

But her cry had been heard. A voice bawled, "Hey! Over here!" and feet came running toward them.

Jonas yanked out the revolver in his belt. Thumping back the hammer, he fired two shots in the direction of the shout. Then he ducked into the icehouse after Susan and slammed the door.

They had been discovered. He had fired the shots only to let the Wileys know it would be wise to keep their distance. Now he pushed Susan to the floor behind the thick log wall, pushed her down into the soft, yielding sawdust. He knelt beside her, his gun still in his hand.

Beyond the door, Sam McCool crouched, his gun also in his hand. The door had sagged open and they could see the gun flashes out there in the darkness fifty yards away.

Bullets thudded into the thick log walls. Splinters, torn from the doorjamb, showered them. Both men shrank back.

A voice yelled, "Come on out with your hands up in the air. Otherwise, we're goin' to kill all of you."

For reply, Jonas leaned forward and loosed a shot in the direction of the voice. He ducked back instantly. He was damned if he was going to give himself up and he sure as hell wasn't going to give Susan up.

Another volley came from the Wileys outside the door. It tore into the sagging door, tore into the thick log walls. Some of the bullets came in, to bury themselves in the sawdust, which was almost three feet deep on the packed earth floor.

They were safe enough for now, Jonas thought, because bullets would not penetrate these thick log walls. But their situation was hopeless. Sooner or later they would have to surrender themselves. There was no other alternative.

Unless the jury back in town brought in a not guilty verdict, he thought. And he didn't see how they could. The jury couldn't even report their verdict to anyone but him.

Outside, the Wileys were yelling back and forth excitedly. At regular intervals, someone emptied a gun into the icehouse walls.

They were like a bunch of kids, he thought, that have cornered an animal or treed a mountain lion.

Chapter 19

At eleven o'clock, the two horses, Jonas's buggy horse and the sheriff's big dappled gray, wandered into town. Neither seemed to have any definite destination. Jonas's buggy horse would eventually have gone home to his stable behind the judge's house. The sheriff's dappled gray would have gone to the livery barn, where he usually was kept.

Tonight, though, there were several horses tied in front of the hotel and across the street in front of the saloon. Farther up the street, a number of horses were tied to hitching posts in front of the courthouse where lights still burned in the upstairs courtroom and in the adjoining jury room. The presence of all these horses in the street drew the two loose horses the way a magnet draws pieces of iron.

Karl Burbach was at the jail, guarding the prisoners, a double-barreled shotgun close at hand. Juan Gallegos had just come out of the saloon. He belched thunderously and pleasurably, then stiffened as the two riderless horses came into the circle of light cast in the street by the windows of the saloon. He yelled, "Hey! What's them horses doin' here? That one's the sheriff's horse!"

John Gebhardt, sitting on the veranda of the hotel, got to his feet and hurried across the street. He said, "And that's the judge's buggy horse!"

Gallegos went to the horses, speaking soothingly. "The reins are tied up." He felt the neck of the dappled gray. "Hair's stiff. He's been rode hard but he's dried off now."

William Clay, whose family was staying temporarily at the hotel because they had no place else, came hurrying across the street. He said in a quietly angry, outraged voice, "By God, this time they've gone too far!"

"You think something's happened to the sheriff and the judge?" Gebhardt asked.

"It looks like it, doesn't it? I'd say the judge and the sheriff went out to the Wiley place to try and get Susan back. They were either killed or taken prisoner.''

Anthony Lambert came out of the saloon, drawn by the commotion in the street. He recognized the sheriff's horse and immediately remembered the coil of rope the sheriff had purchased earlier. He said, ''McCool was in the lumber yard this afternoon. Bought five hundred feet of rope.''

In a shocked voice Gebhardt said, ''Holy Christ! You don't suppose they slid down into that canyon on a rope?''

''It sure does look that way.''

Men now came pouring out of both the saloon and the hotel. Most of the people in town had stayed up late on the chance the jury would bring the verdict in tonight. Doc Fothergill arrived, along with Jake Tipton, Norman Kissick, and David Levinson, who ran the mercantile store. The matter of the riderless horses was discussed several minutes in shocked but excited tones. Men glanced at the courthouse uneasily, as though to reassure themselves that the Wiley brothers were still there waiting for the verdict to be brought in.

A man yelled, ''By God, I say this is just too much! It's time we let the Wileys know they can't do as they damn please!''

The cry was taken up by a dozen other voices. Levinson raised his hands. "Quiet! Do you want the Wiley boys to hear?"

That quieted them. They were angry and they knew something had to be done, but they were not fools.

Gallegos got up on the hitching rail in front of the saloon. "How many of you will join a posse to go out and help the sheriff and the judge?"

This time there was no hesitation. A score of voices replied in the affirmative. Gallegos yelled, "Then go home and get your guns. Get horses too. Come to the courthouse in ten minutes and do it as quietly as you can. There's no use fighting any more Wileys than we have to!"

The crowd dispersed hastily, each man leaving independently. Levinson asked, "What now?"

Gallegos said, "First of all, I think we ought to let the jury know they don't have to be afraid, that they can bring in any verdict they want."

"And what about the Wileys? What will you do about them?"

"They're waiting in the courtroom for the verdict. Let them stay there."

"And the posse?"

"I will take the posse out to the Wiley place."

"How? Those riflemen up in the rocks will mow you down."

"Then they will mow us down. Some of us will get through. Besides, it is dark out there and they will have no time to start fires to light the road."

Levinson said unexpectedly, "I'll get my horse."

Gallegos untied his own horse from the rail in front of the saloon. He swung astride and headed uptown toward the courthouse. The Wileys had cowed and terrified the town by threatening individuals and by singling out Clay and burning his house as an example to others who might resist.

But they'd gone too far when they kidnaped Susan Fuller, when by so doing they'd forced the judge and the sheriff to act. Gallegos wondered if it was possible that Judge Fuller and Sheriff McCool were still alive. He doubted it. If they had survived the descent off the rim, which was unlikely, they would surely have been captured or killed by now. They simply would not be found. Nor would Susan. All three would disappear the way so many others had disappeared inside that valley during the last fifteen or twenty years.

Bill Clay was the first to arrive. He had a double-barreled shotgun in his hands and a nickel-plated revolver stuffed down into his belt, having borrowed both. The others began to arrive shortly afterward. Gallegos stationed them around the courthouse, with orders to shoot any of the Wileys who might come out and fail to halt when ordered to. He cautioned them to be quiet.

Gallegos himself went upstairs. He opened the courtroom door and went in.

Simon raised his head. He had been asleep and he was only mildly curious. The other two remained asleep, stretched out on benches. One of them was snoring lustily.

Gallegos crossed quietly to where Jake Tipton sat in front of the jury room. Jake said, "You can't talk to them. Nobody can."

"But you can. Is that not right?"

Tipton nodded.

"Tell them, then, that they have nothing further to fear from the Wiley family. Tell them there is a posse downstairs and that we are going out to the Wiley place. They can bring in any verdict they please without fear of what may happen to them."

Tipton glanced at Simon and his two

sleeping brothers. "What about them?"

"We will take care of them when we get back. Go in now and tell the jury what I have said."

Grinning, Tipton said, "I'll tell 'em, Juan."

Gallegos turned and hurried from the room, without looking toward the three Wiley brothers. The posse was waiting quietly in the street. He took the reins of his horse from one of them and mounted. He rode up the street at a walk, with the posse following. Only when he reached the edge of town did Gallegos spur his horse.

Out onto the dark Canyon Creek road they thundered. They were several miles from town before they noticed the red glow behind them in the sky. Gallegos knew what it was, and cursed bitterly to himself. He should have seized the Wileys and thrown them into jail. But he hadn't wanted to take the time. He'd figured, they were harmless, at least until a verdict was brought in. Now it looked like he'd been wrong.

Simon watched Gallegos cross the room, saw him whisper briefly to Jake Tipton sitting at the door of the jury room. He saw the way Tipton grinned, saw the way Tipton glanced toward him.

Pretending indifference, he waited until Gallegos had left the courtroom and gone downstairs. Then, stretching lazily, he got up and walked to the window.

He saw the posse in the street. He saw them ride quietly down the street and knew where they were headed. Dropping his air of casualness, he hurried to his brothers and shook them awake. The three went hurriedly out into the hall. Sleepily Andrew asked, "What do you think we oughta do?"

Simon said, "We'd better talk to Pa. There ain't but one place that posse can be goin' to."

Andrew and Thomas agreed. The three hurried downstairs, then down the half-dozen steps to the sheriff's office in the courthouse basement.

Karl Burbach was sitting at the sheriff's desk. He reached for the shotgun leaning against it as they came in, but Simon drew his revolver and said, "Don't."

Burbach let his hand fall to his side. Simon said, "Keys. We want the keys."

Burbach took the keys out of a desk drawer and tossed them to Simon. Simon said, "Watch him," and opened the door leading to the cell block in the rear. He unlocked Solomon's cell first, saying, "There's a posse headed out to our place, Pa. I figured you ought to know."

Solomon came out of his cell. He said, "Let Jude out."

Simon unlocked Jude's cell. The three went back out into the office. Solomon said, "Tie Burbach up."

Simon got handcuffs out of the sheriff's desk. He led Burbach into the cell block. He handcuffed him to the bars. He clipped the deputy over the ear with the barrel of the gun. He didn't even wait for the man to fall. He turned and went back to the office, where his father, Jude, Andrew, and Thomas were waiting for him. Solomon said, "Andrew, you and Thomas go set fire to some buildings. Three or four will do. I don't want any more townspeople coming out to our place tonight."

"What shall we do afterward?"

"Come home."

The two left. Solomon said, "Simon, go down to the livery barn and get three horses. We'll wait here until you get back."

Simon hurried out. He was gone about ten minutes. When he returned, he led the three horses right up to the door. Solomon and Jude came out and mounted up. Simon also mounted and the three rode out of town.

By now, Andrew and Thomas had four fires going. Solomon could hear the fire bell clanging excitedly. People were running in the streets. The town fire engine clattered toward the nearest blaze.

Solomon said, "Come on." This hadn't worked out exactly the way he had planned. He had wanted to get Jude acquitted, and while he might yet succeed in that, he could not twiddle his thumbs in town while a posse attacked his ranch. Jude could help drive the marauders off. Time enough to return him for the jury's verdict after that had been done.

They thundered along the road leading toward their ranch. Behind them the sky glowed red as more fires were started by Thomas and Andrew. Solomon was, in a way, glad that a showdown had finally come. Henceforth, the town would do what he demanded that it do.

He grinned to himself. Luke and his boy would stop that posse in the canyon. They'd pin them down. He and Jude and Simon, coming up behind them, ought to panic them. They'd be damn glad to get back to town. They'd be damn glad to forget all about the judge's girl.

He rode headlong into the narrow canyon, his two sons thundering along behind. He heard the popping of gunfire ahead, and raked his horse repeatedly with his spurs.

Nearing the place where Luke should have been on guard, he felt a sinking sensation in his belly. The shots were too far away. Luke must have been forced to retreat. Or worse, Luke had not even been on guard.

But why? He'd instructed Luke and his boy to guard the canyon road. Why would they disobey? Why would they desert their post?

He didn't know. But for the first time, he felt a touch of fear. Simon had said there were more than twenty men with Juan. Twenty men could do a lot of damage if they wanted to.

The trio thundered past the place where Luke should have been on guard. They pounded on up the road, with the gunfire growing louder as they did. And then Solomon saw what he had feared he might—a red glow in the sky, a red glow that grew stronger rapidly.

They had fired his buildings, he thought. Damn them! He'd make them pay for that!

Recklessly he thundered out of the narrow part of the canyon. He saw half a dozen of his buildings burning in the valley ahead of him. He saw the members of his family running aimlessly back and forth.

A voice called, "Halt! Throw down your guns!"

For reply, Solomon swung the muzzle of the rifle he had taken from the jail toward the voice. He fired, levered in a shell and fired again.

Gunflashes bloomed in a cluster of rocks beside the road. Solomon felt a mighty blow in the middle of his chest. He saw the sky, and then he struck the ground on his back with enough force to drive the breath from him.

He never filled his lungs again. He was as big and as powerful as a grizzly bear. But he had a soft-nosed bullet in his heart.

Chapter 20

Jonas Fuller, Susan, and Sheriff Sam McCool had been in the icehouse only a few minutes when Jonas suddenly heard a man's shouting outside the place. The shooting tapered off and finally it stopped. Luke Wiley's big voice roared, "What you shootin' at?"

"We got the sheriff an' the judge in there!"

"How did they get here?"

Nobody answered that. Jonas grinned faintly to himself. They'd never figure it out. At least they wouldn't until one of them happened to come upon the rope dangling off the rim.

Luke yelled, "Sheriff? Judge? You in there?"

McCool shouted back, "We're here."

"What'd you have to do a damn fool thing like that for? We'd a let your girl go, Judge. Just as soon as Jude got off."

"Jude's not going to get off, Luke."

"Then you ain't goin' to get out of here alive."

Jonas did not reply. He heard Luke say, "Keep 'em there. I got to get back to where I'm supposed to be."

Jonas thought he heard the faint rumble of hoofs. It came as a low, growing thunder in the ground. Luke's horse and that of his son pounded away. Scarcely had they disappeared when a volley of shots popped from the direction of the canyon road. McCool said, "I'll be damned."

Jonas peered cautiously outside. Toward town there was a red glow in the sky, as if the whole town of Canyon Creek was ablaze. In that faint reddish light, he saw a score of milling horses and the flashes of many guns. Luke and his son came galloping back. Luke was yelling, "Take cover. It's a bunch of men from town!"

McCool edged to the door. He took a careful bead on Luke's horse and fired. The animal reared, threw Luke, then fell over on his back. He kicked a few times and then lay still.

Luke got up and sprinted for cover. The others, those that had been outside the icehouse, had disappeared. But the flashes of their guns were visible as they fired at the posse galloping toward them.

Jonas heard Juan Gallegos bawl, "Half a dozen of you stay behind. See that nobody surprises us."

The posse split around the group of buildings from behind which the Wileys were firing. They galloped on, and a few minutes later, Jonas saw the flicker of a growing tongue of flame. The fire must have been started in a hayloft, because it grew like a holocaust. In less than a minute, the whole top of the barn was ablaze.

Those who had taken cover to fight the posse now dropped their guns and ran for the burning building to try and put it out. As though to mock their efforts, another blaze began to grow, this in one of the houses, and a third. The Wileys stopped and stared helplessly.

Luke came from behind a building, shouting, "Don't stand there! Save the house!" He started them running toward the house. He himself ran to the well and began filling buckets. It wasn't going to do any good, Jonas thought. The buildings were all frame and they were jammed close together. One would catch from another. He doubted if there was a chance of saving anything.

Apparently realizing this, Luke turned to face the posse, his rifle in his hands. He fired, and jacked in another cartridge and fired again.

The members of the posse cut loose almost as a single man. Luke doubled as though struck by a giant fist. He started to fall forward, twitching every time a bullet struck. Even after he was on the ground, the bullets continued to slam into him.

McCool was out of the icehouse and running toward the possemen. "Hold your fire! That's enough!"

A man yelled back, "The hell it is! They fired the town after we left! Let's get rid of every goddamned one of 'em while we got the chance!"

Jonas, who had followed McCool, now yelled, "No! Those are women and children. The Wiley men are all in town."

Both McCool and Jonas put themselves deliberately between the posse and the Wileys, who were busily doing what they could to prevent the spread of the flames. Susan, dirty and disheveled, came to stand with her father.

The possemen shuffled unwillingly to their horses. McCool yelled at a couple of them and commandeered their mounts. He swung to the back of one and handed the reins of the other to Jonas. "You and Susan can ride double."

Jonas boosted Susan up. He mounted behind her and followed McCool toward the canyon mouth.

Ahead another volley of shots racketed. McCool had disappeared into the darkness. Jonas said, "Are you all right?"

"I'm all right."

"They didn't hurt you?"

"No." She turned her head and stared at him, her face glowing in the fire's light. "Do you mean to say you and Sam McCool came down that rim on a rope?"

He nodded sheepishly. "We couldn't figure out any other way of getting in. We didn't know the townspeople were going to get mad."

"Is that how you got so dirty and scratched up?"

He nodded. "The rope wasn't long enough."

He thought her face turned pale. The shooting up ahead where the road came out of the canyon had stopped as suddenly

228

as it had begun.

Jonas and Susan reached the place. Jonas could see the huge body of Solomon Wiley lying on the ground. The other Wileys stood in the road, their hands held in the air.

McCool asked, "Who set the fires back in town?"

Nobody replied. McCool said, "All right. Be closemouthed. You can all come with me to jail."

Andrew and Thomas stepped forward. "It was us."

McCool said, "All right. You two and Jude mount up. We're going back."

Jonas looked back as they entered the canyon, riding in single file. Nearly half the Wiley buildings were ablaze. The rest would probably also go. The Wileys would be homeless, at least temporarily.

Most of them would leave, he thought, now that old Solomon was dead. Those who remained would constitute no danger to the community.

He realized suddenly how tired he was. All he wanted was to get home and go to bed.

Fires were still burning in the town of Canyon Creek. Half a dozen houses were completely destroyed. The posse immediately pitched in to help.

John Gebhardt met Jonas and Susan and Sam McCool at the courthouse. He tried to embrace Susan, but she pulled away. Was she disappointed that Gebhardt had not been with the posse that rescued her? Jonas wondered. Or perhaps there had been nothing lasting between them anyway.

Gebhardt hurried away. McCool put Jude Wiley, Andrew and Thomas in the cells. He said, "Jonas, I'll buy you a drink."

"Saloon's not open."

McCool opened the bottom drawer of his desk. He took a bottle out. He rummaged around until he found two glasses, and he poured a drink into each of them.

The two men drank. Susan looked at them. She said, "You're a couple of pretty tough old birds. I think when I get married, I want a man like you."

Jake Tipton came in the door. He said, "The jury's ready, Judge, if you are."

"I'll be right up." He glanced at Sam McCool. "Bring Jude on up."

McCool went back into the cell block after Jude. Jonas looked at Susan. She asked, "How did you instruct the jury?"

"I didn't tell them to bring in a not guilty verdict, if that's what you mean."

She smiled. "That was what I meant."

"You serious about Gebhardt?"

She shook her head.

"Anybody?"

"Not yet."

He nodded, content with her answer. It told him many things—that he was not holding her against her will—that when she found somebody, she would marry him.

They reached the top floor. Jonas let Susan go into the courtroom. He went into his chambers adjoining it.

After a few minutes, Jake Tipton came in. "Ready, Judge?"

"Ready." He got up and followed Tipton into the courtroom. Tipton said, "All rise."

Jonas sat down behind the bench. The jury was sitting in the jury box. He looked at Gus Easley, the foreman. "Have you reached a verdict?"

"We have." Easley handed Tipton a folded piece of paper. He gave it to Jonas, who unfolded it and looked at it. Jonas asked, "How do you find?"

"We find the defendant guilty as charged."

Jonas nodded. He looked at Jude. "Rise and face the court." Normally he would have delayed several days before sentencing. In this case, he thought delay would be unwise.

Jude Wiley got up, cowed and scared for the first time during the trial.

Jonas said, "Jude Wiley, you have been found guilty of the crime of murder in the first degree. Have you anything to say before sentencing?"

Dumbly, Jude shook his head.

Jonas said, not liking this because it was the first death sentence he had ever pronounced, "I sentence you to death by hanging, said sentence to be carried out at the state prison in Cañon City on the 10th day of November. You are remanded to the custody of the sheriff, who will conduct you to the state prison immediately."

Pale and shaken, Jude Wiley collapsed into his chair. Jonas said, "I wish to thank the jury for their courage. Court is adjourned."

His glance met Susan's. He nodded at her, as if to say, "Let's go home."

He retired to his chambers to wait for her. Sam McCool took Jude Wiley downstairs to his cell. The townspeople dispersed.

With some satisfaction, Jonas thought that once more the system had survived. He sat down and waited patiently for Susan to appear.

The publishers hope that this Large Print Book has brought you pleasurable reading. Each title is designed to make the text as easy to see as possible. G. K. Hall Large Print Books are available from your library and your local bookstore. Or you can receive information on upcoming and current Large Print Books and order directly from the publisher. Just send your name and address to:

G. K. Hall & Co.
70 Lincoln Street
Boston, Mass. 02111

or call, toll-free:

1-800-343-2806

A note on the text
Large Print edition designed by
Fred Welden.
Composed in 18 pt English Times
on an Editwriter 7700
by Debra Nelson of G. K. Hall Corp.